ABRIDGED

DAVID
COPPERFIELD

Written by

Charles Dickens

Abridged by

Gita Nath

Illustrated by

Tanoy Choudhury

CONTENTS

PRE-READING ACTIVITIES

1. **A Debate:**
    Organize a debate on the topic:
    'Employing poor children as domestic help is good!'

2. **A Visit with a Purpose**
    Organize a visit to an orphanage. Children must interact with the inmates and must be allowed to share their experiences and emotions. Some gifts and goodies must be taken and distributed.

3. **Group Activity**
    Students must be divided into groups and given time to script the inputs of the orphanage and enact the story to the rest of the students.

4. Find the meanings of the given words and construct sentences:
    vices, inexplicable, benefactors, tranquility, glorious

5. Write synonyms and antonyms of the above words.

6. **Descriptive Writing**
    Write a short note on any one person in your life who has truly influenced you.

7. **Discussion**
    What are your aspirations and how do you plan to realize them.

Chapter 1

I AM BORN

I was born on a Friday, at twelve o'clock at night. The day and hour of my birth made some wise women believe that I was destined to be unlucky in life; and secondly, that I will be able to see ghosts and spirits, simply because I was born towards the small hours on a Friday night. The clock struck twelve and I cried for the first time, announcing my arrival.

Though I never saw my father, for I was born posthumously, yet in my vague memories I remember his white grave-stone in the Churchyard and how that filled me with compassion seeing it lying out alone there in the dark night, when our little parlour was warm and bright with fire and candle.

That Friday, when I was born, my mother was sitting by the fire, unwell and in very low spirits, thinking about the fatherless little stranger, who was ready to arrive in the world. She was very doubtful of coming out alive of the trial that was before her. As she looked through the window, she saw a strange lady coming up the garden. Instead of ringing the bell, she came and looked in, pressing her nose against the glass to such an extent, that it was flat and white. This gave my mother such a shock that she went into labour and I remain indebted to Miss Betsey for having been born on a Friday, at midnight.

My father's aunt Miss Betsey was the principal magnate of our family. My father had once been her favourite but she was very angry by his marriage to 'a wax doll'. Hence, she had never seen my mother. My mother was not yet twenty and my father was double her age when he married. He died a year later, six months before I was born. She was so angry with my father that she did not talk to him after his marriage and my mother had never seen her. Yet she knew it was Miss Betsey for my father would talk about her.

They went into the parlour and they were both seated. My mother was duly inspected by her and after that she stated, 'From the moment of this girl's birth, I intend to be her friend, her godmother, and you'll call her Betsey Trotwood Copperfield. There must be no mistakes in life with this Betsey Trotwood. She must be well brought up and well guarded.

My mother innocently asked what if the baby was a boy. That is impossible said Miss Betsey. By then mother felt so unwell that she called for Peggotty who immediately led her to her own room and dispatched Ham Peggotty, her nephew, to fetch Dr. Chillip.

Dr. Chillip had to spend some anxious moments in the company of Miss Betsey. After a few hours, Dr. Chillip came out of my mother's room with the news of my birth. When it finally registered to Miss Betsey that the new born child was a boy, she did not utter a word, but flung her bonnet at the doctor's face with such displeasure that left the doctor confused. After this, she walked out, never to come back again.

I remember my mother with her long pretty hair and

youthful shape. I also vividly remember Peggotty with no shape at all, with very dark eyes and hard, red cheeks. I remember dancing about in the parlour with my mother, in the winter evenings. She called me 'dear little Davy' and hugged me. We danced, sang songs; she even taught me my lessons when I grew up a bit. I also remember sitting with Peggotty in the parlour. She would do her needlework and I would read to her.

A pleasant evening spent with mother

Chapter 2

A Change in my Life

I was eight years old. Peggotty and I were sitting by the fireplace one night all by ourselves. She was doing some needlework and I was reading to her. My mother was out. Peggotty appeared to me to be a bit occupied. After a while, she hesitatingly asked, 'Master Davy would you like to come along with me and spend a fortnight at my brother's house at Yarmouth? There's the sea, the boats, ships, the fishermen; and the beach! It would be a treat!'

I was thrilled by what I heard. I knew it would be a good treat to live on the seaside but said, 'I don't want to leave Mama alone. She will not allow me!'

'She will as she is also going off on a visit elsewhere. I'm sure she will agree to send you with me!'

Quite contrary to what I thought, my mother agreed to it readily. The day of our departure arrived soon. As the cart was about to leave, my mother stood there hugging me and bidding good bye. Both of us were crying. Mr. Murdstone, whom I had met once while returning from the church was there and he came and stood next to my mother. He seemed annoyed with her tears and said something to her angrily. Both Peggotty and I noticed that and wondered what business was it of his if my mother felt sad seeing me off.

The cart driver, Mr. Barkis was a friendly man. Throughout the trip, Peggotty and he laughed. We ate a good deal and slept a good deal. Finally, the cart reached Yarmouth and when we got into the street it seemed very strange to me and smelt of fish, salt and tar. I saw the sailors walking about, and the carts jingling up and down over the stones. I told Peggotty that I liked the place and she replied saying that it was well-known that Yarmouth was the finest place in the entire universe.

Ham, Peggotty's nephew, met us in the town. He was a huge, strong fellow of six feet high, broad and round-shouldered; but with an innocent boyish face and curly light hair. He lifted me and put me on his shoulder so that I wasn't tired. He held one of boxes under his arm. We turned down lanes and little hillocks of sand, walked past boat-builders' yards, ship-breakers' yards, smiths' forges until we came out upon a flat stretch of land along the sea. Everything seemed new and adventurous to me.

Ham exclaimed, 'There's our house, Master Davy!' I looked in all directions but saw no house. There was a black barge, or some other kind of old boat, not far off, high and dry on the ground, with an iron funnel sticking out of it for a chimney and smoke coming out of it but that did not look like a house to me.

'Where is your house, Ham? That ship like thing? I asked.

'Yes Master Davy! That's the house? That's where we all live! Master Davy!' he exclaimed.

I was charmed with the idea of living in it. We were welcomed by a woman in a white apron. With her was a very beautiful little girl with long yellow curls. Peggotty introduced me, 'This is Mrs. Gummidge, a widow who is my brother's housekeeper and this little girl is Emily, my brother's adopted niece. Like Ham, she is an orphan and my good brother adopted them both at different times.

After a while Mr. Peggotty returned home. I saw that he was a good natured man, as Peggotty had described. I was warmly and affectionately welcomed by him too.

Peggotty showed me my bedroom. It was the most desirable bedroom that I had ever seen. It was in the stern of the vessel with a little window! It had a beautiful mirror framed in oyster shells. Next morning, as soon as the sun rose, I was out of bed and along with little Emily, was on the beach, collecting stones and shells. I told her about my mother and how I love her and will always look after her. She told me that she had lost her father who drowned in the sea. She had even lost her mother. She told me how good and kind Mr. Peggotty was to her and when she grew up she will bring lots of lovely things for him.

I spent most of the fortnight playing together on the beach and going on Ham's boat. Emily told me that she wanted to be a fine lady when she grew up. By the time the fortnight was over, I was quite in love with Emily.

All the time that I had been away from home I did not even once think about my mother. Now that I was returning home the thoughts of mother rushed to my mind. The nearer we drew, the more excited I was to get there and to run into her arms. Peggotty, instead of sharing my excitement, behaved strangely and tried to

At the beach with Little Emily

curtail my enthusiasm. She looked worried and very unlike herself and this confused me.

Finally, when we reached home, the afternoon had turned grey and it was very cold. The sky was dull, threatening rain! I was worried and surprised as Mother wasn't there to greet me.

'Why, Peggotty!' I said, sadly, 'isn't mother home yet?'

'Yes, yes, Master Davy,' said Peggotty. 'She's home. Wait a bit, Master Davy, and I'll tell you something.' She led me to the kitchen.

Before we could reach the kitchen I blurted out, 'Peggotty, I am frightened. 'Why hasn't mama come out to the gate to receive me? Oh, Peggotty! Is she dead, Peggotty?'

Peggotty said, 'Dear, your mama is not dead. She is in good health and she's married again! You have got a new Pa! Come and meet him.' I trembled and turned white.

Peggotty led me by my hand and said, 'Come and see him and your mama!'

We went straight to the parlour, where she left me. On one side of the fire, sat my mother; on the other, Mr. Murdstone. I was surprised to learn that he was now my pa! I had never liked him especially when I saw him last looking displeased with mama. My mother dropped her work and got up to kiss me.

'Now, Clara my dear,' said Mr. Murdstone. 'Remember! Control yourself!'

'Davy boy, how do you do?' I gave him my hand. That was the worst welcome that a child could get when he returns home after a fortnight! I crept upstairs, as soon as I could.

My bedroom had been changed. I was to sleep far away from mama. I was afraid of Mr. Murdstone; in fact I hated him. He intended to reform our lives; my mamas's and mine, with firmness. My mother seemed frightened even to openly love me. My only comfort was with Peggotty in the kitchen. Then, one day Miss Jane Murdstone arrived which made matters worse. On the very first meeting she made it clear that she didn't like me. Soon I began spending time either with Peggotty in the kitchen or in my little bedroom, reading books that had belonged to my father.

Peggotty informed me that there were plans of sending me to a boarding school. Actually, it was Mr. Murdstone and his sister's plan. They wanted me away from mama. I continued learning my lessons at home from my mother. I recited my lessons to mother but that man and his sister were always present. In their presence, I felt so uncomfortable that whatever I learnt left my head. I stuttered and appeared foolish.

One day, I had honestly told him that I couldn't learn while he and his sister sit there watching me. 'You can't, David? Well, let's see!' Mr. Murdstone took me to my room to teach me obedience. He threw me across his lap and hit me heavily with a cane. I cried out in pain and requested him not to beat me but he continued with all severity.

It appeared that he would beat me to death. He had locked the room. I heard my mother and Peggotty crying out to him to spare me but the blows fell again and

Cruel Murdstone thrashes David

again. Nothing seemed to stop his fury. Therefore I could think of nothing else and bit his hand. He was in a wild rage. He threw me to the ground, locked the room from outside and was gone. I was kept a prisoner in my room for five days. I was not permitted to see my mother or Peggotty. On the fifth night, Peggotty came to my door and whispered through the keyhole, 'Master Davy, you are being sent to a boarding near London but don't worry I will take care of your mother!' I was not even allowed to hug my mother before leaving. I looked for Peggotty, but she was not there. I felt very miserable and helpless. Mr. Barkis loaded my box into the cart.

Chapter 3

I'M SENT TO SALEM HOUSE

We might have gone about half a mile when all of a sudden Peggotty emerged from the bushes and climbed in. She took me in both her arms and hugged me. That changed my mood immensely. Mr. Barkis also seemed happier as long as Peggotty was in the coach. Then she gave me some cakes and my mother's purse with some shillings. After another hug, she got down and ran away. That made me a little bit less sad.

During the ride, Mr. Barkis asked me many questions about Peggotty. He seemed very happy when he learnt that Peggotty wasn't married. He asked me to write to her, in my letters that 'Barkis was willing'. At that time I did not understand a thing. It was much later that I understood that he liked Peggotty and wanted to marry her but was too shy to ask her.

Barkis was not supposed to take me to London but drop me midpoint. I was to take another night coach to London. There was no one to receive me. I stood there wondering what to do. I wondered if Mr. Murdstone had devised this plan to get rid of me! Just then a thin young man approached me and asked, 'Are you the new boy?'

He was Mr. Nell, one of the masters at Salem House, the school I was going to. Salem House was a square brick

building of a bare and unfurnished appearance. Mr.
Creakle, the proprietor, I was told by Mr. Nell, was away.
I found it to be the most forlorn place I had ever seen.
Scraps of old copy-books and exercises littered the dirty
floor. There is an unwholesome smell that filled the room.

Mr. Mell left me there. I went to the upper end of
the room where I came upon a pasteboard. It bore these
words: 'WATCH OUT! HE BITES.' When I read this I
assumed that there was a great dog somewhere which
was unfriendly. I looked all round anxiously but I could
not find it. When Mr. Mell came back and saw me looking
around, he asked me what I was looking for.

'I'm looking for the dog that bites.'

'No, Copperfield,' he said gravely, 'that's not a dog.
That's a boy. I have been instructed to put this placard on
your back. I am sorry but I must do it.' With that he tied
the placard, on my shoulders like a knapsack. He told me
that he had been instructed by Mr. Creakle that I had to
carry it wherever I went. It was very humiliating but I had
no choice but to carry it.

Mr. Mell gave me lessons for a month. He was never
harsh. He informed me that I had been sent to school
during the holiday as a punishment. One day, Mr. Mell
informed me that Mr. Creakle was back and I was to
appear before him. He gave me the directions to his
quarters.

Mr. Creakle was a stout gentleman. His face was fiery,
his eyes small and deep set. He had prominent veins on
his forehead, a little nose and a large chin. He was bald

with some thin hair on the sides that was turning grey. He did not look to be a pleasant person at all!

'So!' said Mr. Creakle. 'This is the young gentleman whose teeth are to be filed! Turn him round!' The wooden-legged man, who had escorted me, turned me to show him the placard.

'I know your step father! He is a worthy man with a strong character,' spoke Mr. Creakle, pinching my ear with ferocious playfulness.

'Sir,' I faltered, 'can you allow me to get this writing removed before the boys come back?'

Mr. Creakle sprang out of his chair with so much ferocity, that I ran and did not stop until I reached my own bedroom. I went to bed and lay trembling for a couple of hours.

Chapter 4

MY FIRST TERM AT SALEM HOUSE

Traddles arrived before the rest of the boys and I was fortunately saved from the embarrassment of either disclosure or concealment. He presented me to every other boy on their return. I was not considered as being formally received into the school, until J. Steerforth arrived. He was reputed to be a great scholar. I was taken to him as if he were a magistrate. He was very good-looking and very senior to me.

He told me that it was the tradition of the school for a new boy to treat others to a secret feast.

I emptied the purse that Peggotty had given me into Steerforth's hand. At night the boys sat eating and talking in whispers. The moonlight was streaming into the room which gave it a certain mysterious atmosphere. I listened to all they told me with awe. They talked about ghosts and I was very scared though I pretended not to be. The boys also narrated stories about the school and the masters.

'Good night, young Copperfield,' said Steerforth. 'I'll take care of you.' I replied gratefully. 'I am very much obliged to you.' I began to adore Steerforth more than I did earlier.

Boys at Salem House feasting at midnight

Chapter 5

RETURNING HOME FOR THE VACATION

The school began in right earnestness from the next day. I remember how the roar of voices in the schoolroom suddenly became hushed as death when Mr. Creakle entered and stood in the doorway looking upon us like a giant in a story-book surveying his captives.

Mr. Creakle really enjoyed his profession as he took immense delight in hurting the boys. Steerforth proved a very useful friend. It was because he took me under his patronage that nobody dared to annoy me. However, he couldn't defend me from Mr. Creakle. One day, after he watched how roughly I was treated by Mr. Creakle, Steerforth advised me that I should start standing up for myself.

The idea that the holidays were far changed as the day began to inch closer. From counting months, we started counting weeks, and then days. I had this fear that I might not be sent for by Mr. Murdstone but when I learnt from Steerforth that I was certainly going home. I was relieved. Finally, we all got into the coach which stopped at mid point where Barkis had dropped me. Mr. Barkis was there to collect me.

'Good morning, Mr. Barkis! You look very well!
I greeted him. Mr. Barkis said nothing by way of

acknowledging the compliment. That was not the cheerful Mr. Barkis that I knew. So I told him, 'I gave your message to Peggotty, Mr. Barkis,'

'Ah!' said Mr. Barkis, drily. 'When a man says he's willing, he is waiting for an answer.'

'Did you tell Peggotty so, Mr. Barkis?' I asked.

'No!' growled Mr. Barkis. 'I can't tell her myself!' He sat quietly pondering for a while. 'Well!' he resumed at length. 'Tell Peggotty that Barkis is waiting for an answer.'

Chapter 6

MY HOME COMING

It was a strange feeling to be going home. On one hand I remembered the happy old home, of which I could never dream again, the days when my Mother, I and Peggotty were together! On the other hand, was the thought of the cruel Murdstones who had made me a stranger in my own home. I was not sure whether I was glad or not to return!

Mr. Barkis put my box down at the garden-gate and left. No one was there to receive me. That added greatly to my confusion. I walked along the path towards the house, glancing at the windows, and fearing at every step to see Mr. Murdstone or Miss Murdstone. Fortunately, they were not there! I opened the door, without knocking, I went in quietly and timidly as if I was stealing into someone's house.

God knows how happy I was to hear my mother's voice. I remember listening to her singing to me when I was a baby. Since I entered the room very quietly she did not hear or see me come. She was sitting by the fire, suckling an infant.

When I spoke to her, she was startled and cried out, 'Oh dear Davy!' She kissed and hugged me warmly.

'He is your brother,' said my mother, pointing to

the baby. 'Davy, my lovely son! My poor child!' Then she kissed and hugged me again. While mother was showering her affection on me, Peggotty came running in, and was delirious with joy to see me!

I had arrived before I was expected. Mr. and Miss Murdstone had gone out to visit a neighbour, and would not return before night. I had never dreamt that that we three were together, undisturbed, once more and I felt, as happy as in the past. We dined together by the fireside. Mother made Peggotty dine with us. While we were eating, I told Peggotty what Mr. Barkis had asked me to tell her. She began to laugh and, in embarrassment, she threw her apron over her face.

'Oh, that man!' cried Peggotty, 'he wants to marry me!'

'It would be a very good match for you; wouldn't it?' said my mother.

'I don't know,' said Peggotty. 'Don't ask me. I haven't ever thought of marriage!'

While we continued with our dinner, I noticed that mama had become serious and thoughtful. Her face was still very pretty but she looked careworn and weak.

We sat round the fire and talked delightfully. I told them about Mr. Creakle and how harsh he was. I also told them what a fine fellow Steerforth was. I took the little baby in my arms when it was awake and cooed to it lovingly. I crept close to my mother's side according to my old custom and sat with my arms round her waist. I was very happy indeed.

That evening was the only happy time of my stay. Miss Murdstone barred me from dining with mama and

Peggotty and I was prohibited from holding my baby brother. One month passed like this where I lived in extreme hostility and coldness. I resolved to keep myself as much out of their way as I could. Sometimes, in the evenings, I went and sat with Peggotty in the kitchen. Otherwise, I spent most of my time in my bedroom, pouring over a book. My mother looked sad but could not do much.

Soon, it was time for me to depart. I must confess that I was not unhappy to leave. The only thing that left me sad was leaving Mama and Peggotty at the garden gate.

I had got into the coach and the coach had begun to move when I heard her calling to me. I looked out and saw her. She stood at the garden-gate alone, holding her baby up in her arms for me to see and looking intently at me. That is how I saw her in my dreams at school. Little did I realise then that that was the last time I was seeing my baby brother and mother alive!

David's last look at his mother

Chapter 7

BEREAVED

Two months later, I was summoned by Mrs. Creakle. It was my tenth birthday. I thought Peggotty had sent me a gift. Mrs. Creakle held a letter in her hand. She looked very concerned when she asked me, 'Was your mother well when you last visited her? Before I could understand what she was asking, she falteringly, added, 'I'm very sorry, David, that your mother and brother have died!'

I cried the whole day and felt like an orphan. I thought of my father's grave in the churchyard and of my mother lying there, beside him. She looked after me tenderly till I was sent home in a coach.

Once I reached home, I ran into Peggotty's arms and cried my heart out. Her grief burst out when she saw me; but she controlled herself and spoke in whispers, and walked softly, as if the dead would be disturbed. She looked very tired and sad. She told me that she was at my mother's bedside, day and night, during her last days.

Mr. Murdstone took no heed of me when I went to him. I felt lost and lonely. I stood crying at my mother's grave. He looked concerned and sad but did not console me at my great loss.

Later Peggotty told me, ' Your mama was unwell
for a long time. She was uncertain and unhappy. When
her baby was born, I thought that she would get better,
but she would brood and cry. Every hard word was like
a blow to her. The last time that I saw her like her own
old self, was the night when you came home. The day
you left for school, she said to me, 'I shall never see my
darling son again. Something tells me so! I know!' shared
Peggotty among sobs. 'She never told her husband what
she told me. One night, a little more than a week before it
happened, she said, 'I think I am dying! Sit by me while I
sleep; don't leave me. God bless and protect my fatherless
boy!'

Chapter 8

BARKIS MARRIES PEGGOTTY

After the funeral, the first thing that Miss Murdstone did was to dismiss Peggotty. Peggotty tried to find a job for herself but had failed and therefore, had decided to return to Yarmouth. I mustered courage and asked Miss Murdstone if I could be allowed to go to Yarmouth with Peggotty. She permitted me not because that would make me happy but because she wished to get rid of me. I even asked her when I was going back to school. She answered dryly that I was not going to school any more. That made me extremely anxious. I wanted to know what was going to be done with me. When I shared this with Peggotty, she was equally concerned. We set out for Yarmouth as we did in the past in Mr. Barkis' coach. He was very happy and grinned at Peggotty all the way to Yarmouth.

Mr. Peggotty and Ham received me very warmly. I was amazed to see Emily who had grown. She had started going to school. She had become prettier and livelier. When I wanted to kiss her, she covered her cherry lips with her hands, and said she wasn't a baby anymore and ran into the house, laughing. She was affectionate, sweet-natured and had such a pleasant manner of being both sly and shy at once. She captivated me more than ever.

Unlike the past, Emily and I seldom wandered on the beach. She had tasks to learn and needle-work to do. I realized that we would not have had those old wanderings because we were no longer children.

One day, Peggotty and Mr. Barkis took Emily and me for a ride. I was very happy at the prospect of spending the entire day with Emily. Mr. Barkis wore a new blue coat but Peggotty was dressed as usual in her neat dress. He stopped at a church. Mr. Barkis, along with Peggotty, went in, leaving Emily and me alone in the chaise. I took that occasion to propose to Emily. She consented and allowed me to kiss her. When Mr. Barkis and Peggotty came out of the church, Mr. Barkis informed us that they were married. He was beaming with joy but Peggotty was shy and blushing.

After dropping Emily and me to the boathouse, Mr. and Mrs. Barkis bade us good-bye, and drove away to their own home. Next morning she returned and after breakfast she took me to her own beautiful little home. She told me that there will always be a special room in her house for me with the crocodile book on the table and that I will always be welcome to stay there with them. I was truly touched by her warm gesture.

My stay at Yarmouth came to an end. I thanked everyone and left. Barkis and Peggotty came to drop me. They left me at the gate. It was a strange sight to see the cart taking Peggotty away and leaving me under the old elm-trees looking at the house, in which there was no face that had a trace of warmth or love. I felt that I did not belong there.

I fell into a state of neglect. The Murdstones disliked me. They sullenly, sternly and steadily ignored me. I was not beaten or starved but was coldly neglected.

Mr. Barkis marries Peggotty

I was seldom allowed to visit Peggotty. Faithful to her promise, she either came to see me, or met me somewhere near, once every week and never empty-handed.

One day, Mr. Murdstone said to me, 'David, you know that I am not rich. As you have already received considerable education, it would be futile to keep you at school. Mr. Quinion looks after my warehouse and is willing to employ you. You will earn enough to provide for your meals and pocket-money. I have arranged for your lodging with a family. That will be paid by me. You are going to London to begin the world on your own account.'

I was convinced now that Mama and Peggotty were gone, it was my turn next. It was a plan to get rid of me. It neither pleased nor frightened me. I was more confused than ever. I was a mere ten- year old. I had been told to leave the next day to work in London.

Peggotty and David share some tender moments

Chapter 9

A WORKER IN A WAREHOUSE

Murdstone and Grinby's warehouse was at the waterside. It was an old dilapidated house, overrun with rats and full of dirt, gathered over a hundred years. Murdstone and Grinby's trade was the supply of wines and spirits to certain ships. I had to wash, rinse and label wine bottles. Then, I had to fit corks, reject damaged bottles and pack finished bottles in casks.

At half past twelve, Mr. Quinion called me to his office and I was introduced to Mr. Micawber, middle aged man who wore shabby clothes. 'This,' said Mr. Quinion, pointing to me, 'is Master Copperfield!'

'Mr. Murdstone wants me to take you in as a lodger. I will come here in the evening and show you the shortest route between the warehouse and the lodging'.

At the appointed time in the evening, Mr. Micawber reappeared. We walked to the house, together; Mr. Micawber telling me the name of streets and landmarks so that I might find my way in the morning.

The house, Windsor Terrace was equally shabby. Mrs. Micawber, a thin lady, was sitting in the parlour with their four tiny children. The first floor was unfurnished. The blinds were kept down to fool neighbours and creditors. My room was at the top of the house. It was scantily and very poorly furnished.

Despite the miserable living conditions, the Micawbers were kind to me. At times they invited me to share their hot dinner. They even let me sit near the fireplace on cold nights. My petty allowance could merely afford a penny loaf and a pennyworth of milk. Often, I went to bed hungry. I was lonely and frightened.

My rescue from this kind of existence seemed impossible. I was convinced that I will never reconcile to it and would always remain miserable. Many letters passed between Peggotty and me but I did not mention my suffering even to her, partly because I did not want to upset her and partly for shame. I was made to live in the most inhuman conditions.

Mr. Micawber had problems with the debtors. Creditors visited him at all hours; some of them were very harsh. The Micawbers began selling and pawning their movables. One day, he was arrested and put in prison till he could clear his debts. His family was permitted to live there with him. Mrs. Micawber found a cheap room for me near the prison but I did not want to live there all by myself. They cared for me but they themselves were helpless.

David driven to poor Micawbers' home

Chapter 10

I RUN AWAY TO DOVER

I resolved to run away to the only relative I had in the world, Miss Betsey. I decided to tell her my story and ask her for help. I wrote to Peggotty and asked her for Aunt Betsey's address. I even asked her to lend me a half-guinea which I promised to repay.

Peggotty's answered soon and was, as usual, full of affection. She enclosed the half- guinea and told me that Miss Betsey lived near Dover but where exactly in Dover, she did not know. After making a few enquiries about the place, I resolved to set out. I paid a man to take me and my box of clothing on his cart but the man drove off with my money and the box. I ran after the cart but was left panting and crying, with only five shillings to get me to Dover. I walked, slept under haystacks or in the fields at night.

At the end of six days, famished, tired and utterly dirty, I stumbled into Dover. My shoes were torn; my hair was dirty and uncombed. It was in this state that I reached Miss Betsey's house. It was a neat little cottage on a cliff overlooking the sea. I remembered hearing that she was a stern lady. Hence; I did not have the courage to knock at the door. I waited till a tall, grey- haired lady came out. When she saw me, she cried, 'Go away! No boys are allowed here!'

David reaches Aunt Betsey's Home

I gathered courage and said, 'Aunt Betsey, I am your nephew, David Copperfield of Blunderstone, in Suffolk. I used to hear my mother talk about you before she died! I blurted out all that I had to tell her. I told her that I have been ill treated since then. So I ran away to my only relative! I was sent to work in a warehouse not fit for me. I was robbed and have walked all the way from London to Dover. I have never slept in a bed since I began the journey.' Having said all this very quickly, I broke down into uncontrollable sobs.

'Oh my God!' said my aunt. She took me inside and made me drink some restoratives but I continued to be hysterical. She put me on the sofa bundled up in three shawls.

She called Janet, her servant and asked her to call Mr. Dick. She wanted to consult him about how she should handle this situation.

Janet was confused but went on her errand. My aunt paced the room restlessly till Mr. Dick arrived. He was a pleasant-faced man with bright, gay eyes.

'Mr. Dick, I want your advice! This is David Copperfield, my late nephew's son. He has run away. What shall I do with him?' she asked.

'Why, I would wash him and then feed him. Possibly some rest would be good after that,' he replied.

When I bathed, Janet and Aunt put me in Mr. Dick's shirt and trousers. Then, Janet tied me up in two-three shawls. I lay down on the sofa. Being very exhausted, I fell asleep without my realizing it.

Soon after waking up, we had our dinner. I told Aunt Betsey about my mother's unfortunate wedding with Mr. Murdstone and the way he and his sister, ill treated my mother and me. All the while, I was very worried to know what she was planning to do with me. We had our dinner in complete silence, except when she occasionally said, 'Mercy upon us!'

After dinner, Aunt Betsey and Janet took me to a cosy bedroom. It was a pleasant one, at the top of the house, overlooking the sea, on which the moon was shining brilliantly. I heard them lock my door on the outside. She might have suspected that I had a habit of running away, and took precautions, on that account, to have me in safe keeping.

Chapter 11

AUNT BETSEY WRITES TO
MR. MURDSTONE

I slept peacefully after a long time. Next morning, my aunt told me that she had written to Mr. Murdstone, whom she called 'murderer'.

'Does he know where I am? Will I have to go back to him?' I asked alarmed.

'I don't know! We shall see. Now you go upstairs and say good morning to Mr. Dick,' she told me.

My spirits sank! I found Mr. Dick busy with the manuscript. He was so engrossed in it, that I had enough time to observe the large paper kite in a corner, bundles of manuscript and a large number of pens.

Mr. Dick put down his pen and said, 'Do you know how the world goes? I'll tell you,' and he put his lips close to my ear. 'It's a mad world. Mad as Bedlam, boy!' Then he began laughing heartily. He showed me his kite and promised that we will fly it. He pointed to me that it was covered with manuscript, very closely and laboriously written. As I looked along the lines, I saw some allusion to King Charles the First's head, in one or two places.

'There's plenty of string,' said Mr. Dick, 'and when it flies high, it takes the facts a long way. That's my manner of diffusing them. I don't know where the kites may come down'. I was not sure if that he was joking with me. So I laughed and he laughed and we parted as good best friends.

The next few days were filled with so much of happiness that I forgot my miserable past. Mr. Dick and my aunt were very kind to me. In my happiness, I even forgot that my aunt had written to Mr. Murdstone and called him over to meet her.

At length, Mr. Murdstone replied to my aunt. She informed me that he was coming to meet her, the next day. This news filled me with infinite terror. I dreaded even looking at the face of the cruel Mr. Murdstone.

Chapter 12

THE VISITORS I DREADED

Next morning, I found that my aunt was sterner than usual in receiving the visitor whom I dreaded. She sat near the window. I would have given anything to disappear from there but Aunt Betsey insisted that I stayed. So, I stood there, in a corner, frightened and nervous.

Mr. Murdstone, along with his sister, walked in. Without any courtesies being exchanged, he began with his well prepared speech, 'I must tell you, Miss Trotwood that David has troubled us a lot, as he is troubling you now by running away. He is stubborn, rude and has a violent temper,' stated Mr. Murdstone.

'Rubbish!' cried Miss Betsey. 'I don't believe a word you say. You are murderers! Your cruelty caused his mother's death. You sent a ten-year old boy to earn his living while you lived comfortably in a house that belongs to David, now that his mother is dead! Why did he not run away when his mother was alive? If the poor child's mother had been alive, would you have treated him in this manner?' said my aunt.

'Clara, God bless her soul, would dispute nothing which I or my sister decided was for the best!' he replied, haughtily and with a sense of misplaced confidence.

'Humph!' said my aunt. 'Poor baby, she wouldn't have had a choice! 'Your late wife, sir, was very innocent, a little baby herself!' returned my aunt. 'And now, what have you got to say next?'

'Merely this, Miss Trotwood,' he returned. 'I am here to take David back unconditionally and deal with him as I think right. I am not here to make any promise or give any pledge to anybody. I cannot trifle or be trifled with. I am here, for the first and last time, to take him away. If he decides not to go now, my doors are shut against him for ever!'

'What does David have to say?' said my aunt.

'Please Aunt Betsey! Don't send me with them. Neither of them has ever liked me or been kind to me. They made Mama and Peggotty unhappy too. I was very miserable! Please protect me for my parents' sake and don't send me away with them!' I pleaded.

Mr. Dick's face brightened immediately and he rejoined, 'Have him measured for a suit of clothes right away.'

'Mr. Dick,' said my aunt triumphantly, 'Give me your hand, for your advice is invaluable.' Having shaken it with great cordiality, she pulled me towards her for a warm embrace and then said to Mr. Murdstone, 'You may leave! I'll take my chance with the boy but I don't believe a word you said!'

Once the Murdstones left, I ran to Aunt Betsey and flung my arms around her and hugged her. My eyes were filled with tears and my heart with gratitude. Then I went to Mr. Dick and thanked him most sincerely.

*Mr. Dick, Aunt Betsey and David celebrate after
Murdstones leave*

Chapter 13

A NEW LIFE

Aunt Betsey insisted on calling me Trotwood
Copperfield. I had two new guardians with
hearts of gold. She purchased some ready-made clothes
that afternoon which she marked 'Trotwood Copperfield',
in her own handwriting and in indelible marking-ink. I
began my new life, with a new name and with everything
new about me.

My friendship and intimacy with Mr. Dick grew as
time passed. At the same time, my aunt grew so fond of
me that, in the course of a few weeks, she shortened my
adopted name of Trotwood into Trot. She told me that if I
remained as good as I was then; I will always be loved as
much.

'Trot,' said my aunt one evening, 'we must not forget
your education.'

I felt quite delighted when she referred to it as even
I wanted to educate myself. She suggested that I go to
school in Canterbury for which I willingly agreed.

'Very good, then!' said my aunt. 'Janet, hire the grey
pony and chaise tomorrow morning at ten o'clock, and
pack up Master Trotwood's clothes tonight.'

I was greatly elated by this development but I was sad
to see its effect on Mr. Dick, who was very low-spirited at

the prospect of our separation. Next morning, we parted in the most affectionate manner.

My aunt, completely indifferent to public opinion, drove the grey pony herself, through Dover in a masterly manner. When she asked me whether I was happy, I told her that I was truly happy and excited about going to school.

She was much gratified and patted me on the head. She told me that we were going to meet Mr. Wickfield, her lawyer who would advise her on the school which was the best for me. At length we stopped before a very old house with long low lattice-windows. The house seemed to be leaning onto the road.

'Is Mr. Wickfield at home, Uriah Heep?' said my aunt.

'Mr. Wickfield's at home, ma'am,' said Uriah Heep, 'please walk in!'

Just then, a door at the farther end of the room opened and a gentleman entered.

'Miss Betsey Trotwood!' said the gentleman, 'please walk in. I was engaged for a moment, but you'll excuse my being busy.'

Miss Betsey acknowledged his greeting and we went into his room, which was furnished as an office with books, papers. It looked into a beautiful and well kept garden.

'Well, Miss Trotwood,' said Mr. Wickfield, what brings you here?'

'This is my nephew, David Copperfield. I plan to put

him in a good school where he will be taught and treated well! I need your help in choosing such a school.'

Mr. Wickfield suggested Dr. Strong's school for boys. It was a good school and when we went to the school to see it and meet Dr. Strong, my aunt approved it immediately. Since it was not a boarding school, Mr. Wickfield offered to let me live in his home for the weekdays as I would spend my weekends with Aunt Betsey.

'I am very much obliged to you,' said my aunt; 'and so is he, but...I wish to....'

'I know what you mean,' cried Mr. Wickfield. 'You may pay for him if you like. We won't be hard about terms but if you must insist you could pay.'

'On that understanding,' said my aunt, 'though it doesn't lessen the real obligation, I shall be very glad to leave him.'

I was introduced to Mr. Wickfield's daughter, Agnes, a happy, cheerful girl who would be my age. She possessed tranquillity beyond her years. When I saw how Mr. Wickfield held her hand, I understood that both were very fond of each other.

We went upstairs to see the room. It was a glorious room. My aunt was as happy as I was with the arrangement made for me.

'Trot,' said my aunt in conclusion, 'be a credit to yourself, to me and Mr. Dick! Then, even Heaven be with you! Never be mean; never be false; never be cruel. Avoid these three vices, Trot, and I can always be hopeful of you,' said my aunt.

I was greatly overcome and could only thank her, again and again and send my love to Mr. Dick. I promised her that I would never abuse her kindness or forget her advice. She embraced me and left so that she could reach home before dark. When I looked out of the window, I saw how dejectedly she got into the chaise and drove away, without looking up.

Next morning, Mr. Wickfield took me to school and introduced me to my new master, Dr. Strong. The school was excellent, totally different from my previous school. Dr. Strong was knowledgeable and an excellent teacher. He was kind to all boys. The boys loved and respected him. I overcame my uneasiness gradually. In less than a fortnight I was quite at home and happy among my new companions. I was still a bit awkward in their games and fairly backward in studies. I worked very hard, both in sports and studies and soon, I gained commendation. I was very happy and felt settled but, for some inexplicable reason, the presence of Uriah Heep would always disturb me.

Chapter 14

VISITING OLD FRIENDS

My childhood has given way to my youth! I am seventeen and the Head Boy of the school. Doctor Strong refers to me in public as a promising young scholar. Mr. Dick is wild with joy, and my aunt remits me a guinea by the next post. Everyone is very happy at my progress! Agnes, my counsellor and friend has also grown into a charming, young and poised woman.

It was time to leave school and Dr. Strong. I had learnt a lot and had been very happy! I was distinguished in that little world. I also thought of the promising future that awaited me.

My aunt and I had serious discussions about my career. I was undecided and had no particular preference for any career. My aunt suggested that I take a break of a month, explore the possibilities and then decide. It will help me to know my mind, and form a cooler judgement.

She suggested that I could first visit Peggotty and London after that.

'It's a mercy that your mother didn't live,' said my aunt, looking at me approvingly. 'She would have been so proud of her boy at this time. Trotwood, how much you remind me of her!'

'He is so much like David!' added Mr. Dick.

I was given substantial amount of money and tenderly sent off on my expedition. While parting, my aunt advised me and sent me off with many kisses. I was at liberty to do what I wanted, for three weeks or a month; and no other conditions were imposed upon my freedom than a pledge to write three times a week and faithfully report myself.

I went to Canterbury first, that I might take leave of Agnes and Mr. Wickfield. With a heavy heart, I packed my clothes and books to be sent to Dover. Agnes was very glad to see me. She shared with me that she was worried about her father. His hands trembled, his speech was shaky and he often had a wild look. We had tea with Doctor Strong. He made much of my going away as if I were going to China and treated me as an honoured guest.

I set out for London and as I passed by Salem House, I wanted to go in and meet Mr. Creakle, return all his thrashings and let out all the boys caged there. I even looked out for those places where I had rested during my weary journey to Dover.

The coach had stopped overnight at an inn at Charing Cross. As I sat in the coffee room, a handsome well-formed young man dressed with a tasteful easy negligence which I recognized instantly, appeared and I called out to him, 'Steerforth, won't you speak to me?'

He looked at me but he did not recognize me.

'You don't remember me?' I asked.

'My God!' he exclaimed surprised. 'It's little Copperfield!'

We shook hands most warmly as I was overjoyed to see him. We sat together and I told him all that had happened with me ever since I left Salem House. He told me that he was a student at Oxford University and was on his way home.

I told Steerforth that I was going to visit the Peggottys and asked him if he would like to join. He agreed but suggested that if I wasn't in a hurry, we could stop at his home at Highgate, for a few days and then go to Yarmouth. So, we decided to head for Highgate.

At dusk, the stage-coach stopped with us at an old brick house on the summit of the hill, in Highgate.

I was introduced to Mrs. Steerforth, an elderly lady with a handsome and authoritative face. She extended a warm welcome to me.

It was a genteel old-fashioned house, very quiet and orderly. From the windows of my room I saw all London lying in the distance. Soon we were called for dinner.

There was another lady in the dining-room. She attracted my attention, perhaps because of something really remarkable in her. She had black hair and eager black eyes. She was introduced as Miss Dartle, and both Steerforth and his mother, called her Rosa. She lived there and had been for a long time Mrs. Steerforth's companion.

There was a servant in that house, Littimer, who was mostly with Steerforth, and had come into his service at the University. I had never seen a more respectable-looking man. He was taciturn, deferential and observant.

A week passed by rapidly in the most delightful

manner. This stay gave me many occasions for knowing Steerforth better which increased my admiration for him.

Finally, it was time for us to depart. He had been doubtful at first whether to take Littimer or not, but decided to leave him at home. We bade adieu to Mrs. Steerforth and thanked Miss Dartle for her hospitality and kindness.

We reached Yarmouth late in the night and checked into a hotel. Next morning, I found that Steerforth had been strolling about the beach before I woke up and had made acquaintance with half the boatmen in the place. Moreover, he told me that he was sure that he had seen the house of Mr. Peggotty.

I decided that we would visit Mr. Peggotty's family in the evening, when they are all sitting round the fire.

I suggested to Steerforth that we must take them by surprise!

'Now, you are going to see your nurse, I suppose?'

'Why, yes,' I said, 'I must see Peggotty first of all.'

I gave him minute directions for finding the residence of Mr. Barkis, and we decided that he would reach in two hours.

There was a sharp bracing air; the sea was crisp and clear; the sun was diffusing abundance of light and everything was fresh and lively. The streets looked small. The streets that we have only seen as children always do, when we go back to them. Nothing had changed.

I went to meet my dear old Peggotty. She was cooking dinner! When I knocked at the door she opened it, and asked me what I wanted. I smiled at her but she did not recognize me. I had been writing to her but I was meeting her after seven years.

'I want to ask about a house in Blunderstone, that they call the Rookery,' said I.

She looked at me again and exclaimed, 'My darling boy, Master Davy!'

'Peggotty!' I cried and we both burst into tears and were locked in one another's arms.

'Barkis will be so glad,' said Peggotty, wiping her eyes with her apron,

'Will you come up and see him, my dear?'

He received me with absolute enthusiasm. He was too rheumatic but we talked about the time when Barkis was willing but too shy to tell Peggotty.

I prepared Peggotty for Steerforth's arrival and it was not long before he came. She knew no difference between his having been a personal benefactor of hers, and a kind friend to me, and that she would have received him with the utmost gratitude and devotion in any case.

However, his easy, spirited good humour and his handsome looks, his natural gift of adapting himself, bound her to him wholly in five minutes. At eight in the evening, we started for the boat house to meet Mr. Peggotty, Emily and Ham. The door was unlatched and we decided to get in stealthily and give them all a pleasant surprise. Mr. Peggotty sat by the fire, his face beaming with happiness. Emily and Ham sat opposite to him, holding hands and Mrs. Gummidge was clapping

A happy reunion: Peggotty and David

her hands, most excitedly. The very next moment Emily's eyes caught us and Ham cried out excitedly, 'It's Master Davy!'

In a moment we were all shaking hands and asking one another how we did, and telling one another how glad we were to meet, and all talking at once. Mr. Peggotty was so overjoyed to see us that he did not know what to say or do. His face simply beamed with happiness.

Ham told us shyly that he and Emily are getting married. We congratulated them and talked and laughed as Steerforth narrated stories. Steerforth was also very impressed with the warmth and love they extended to us.

Steerforth and I stayed for more than a fortnight in Yarmouth. He was a good sailor and accompanied Mr. Peggotty when he went fishing. I generally remained with Peggotty. I liked to revisit the old and familiar scenes of my childhood at Blunderstone. I had no idea how he engaged himself while I was away.

I visited our old home which I hadn't seen for seven years .There were changes in my old home. Many trees had been chopped off. The garden had run wild, and half the windows of the house were shut. It appeared that no one was living there. The graves of my parents were overgrown with grass and they filled me with extreme sadness.

One dark evening, I found Steerforth alone in Mr. Peggotty's boat house, sitting thoughtfully before the fire. He was so engrossed in his own thoughts that he did not see me approach.

I stood there for a while when he noticed me. There were dark clouds on his forehead. The he spoke, 'I was thinking of these people we found so glad on the night of our coming down, who might come to some harm. David, I wish to God that I had been better guided!' he exclaimed. He was completely unlike himself.

'I have taken a fancy to the place. I have bought a boat that was for sale, a clipper. Mr. Peggotty will master her in my absence. Littimer will come down and get the sails fitted and get the boat renamed. I am calling her, 'Little Emily! Did I tell you Littimer had come down? He came down this morning, with a letter from my mother.'

As our looks met, I observed that he was pale even to his lips, though he looked very steadily at me. I feared that some difference between him and his mother might have led to his being in that frame of mind.

I received a letter from my aunt. I wanted to discuss it with Steerforth on the journey home. We took leave of all our friends. Mr. Barkis was very upset and would have sacrificed a guinea to keep us there for some more time.

Mr. Peggotty's entire family was very sad at our departure. The entire family of Omer and Joram, who had prepared a coffin for my mother, and the funeral suit for me and, whom I had befriended earlier, came to bid us good-bye. In short, when we departed, we left behind many people in a sad state of mind.

For some little time we held no conversation, Steerforth being unusually silent, and I being engrossed in thinking when I should see them all again. Soon

Steerforth said, 'Find a voice, David. What were you telling about your Aunt's letter at breakfast?'

'Why, she reminds me, Steerforth,' said I, 'that I came out on this expedition to explore and to think what profession I wish to pursue.'

'To tell you the truth, I had completely forgotten about the objective of the mission,' I added.

'What does your aunt have in mind?' inquired Steerforth, glancing at the letter in my hand. 'Does she suggest anything?'

'Yes! She has asked me if I should like to be a proctor? What do you think of it? 'What is a proctor, Steerforth?' I. asked.

Steerforth told me all that he knew about proctors and that occupation.

I quite made up my mind to do so. I told Steerforth that my aunt was in town waiting for me. She had taken lodgings for a week at a kind of private hotel at Lincoln's Inn Fields. When we came to our journey's end, I drove to Lincoln's Inn Fields. We were very pleased to meet again. My aunt was very happy to see me and embraced me with immense affection. After supper, she began, 'Well, Trot, what do you think of the proctor plan? Or have you not begun to think about it yet?'

'I have thought a good deal about it, my dear aunt, and even talked about it with Steerforth. I like it very much indeed. '

'That's heartening!' said my aunt.

'I have only one concern, aunt. From what I understand, it is a limited profession, and my entrance into it would be very expensive?"

'It will cost just a thousand pounds.' returned my aunt.

'My dear aunt, it's a large sum of money. You have spent a great deal on my education, and have always been liberal to me. Surely there are some other ways in which I might begin my professional life without this sort of expenditure!

My aunt looked at me full in the face and replied, 'Trot, my child, I have one objective in life. It is to provide for your being a good, a sensible and a happy man. I am bent upon it and so is Dick. It's in vain, Trot, to recall the past! Perhaps I might have been better friends with your father and your mother. When you came to me, a little runaway boy, all dusty and way-worn, I thought so. From that time until now, Trot, you have been a credit to me and a pleasure. You are my adopted child. Only be a loving child to me in my old age and bear with my whims and fancies is all that I would hope for!'

It was the first time I had heard my aunt refer to her past history. There was magnanimity in her quiet way of doing so. It exalted her in my respect and affection.

'All is agreed and understood between us, now, Trot,' said my aunt,' 'and we need talk of this no more. Give me a kiss and we'll go to the Commons, tomorrow.'

Next morning, we set out for the office of Spenlow and Jorkins, my aunt's proctors. They had an opening for a proctor- in-training and agreed to take me on a month's trial.

Then we set out for Buckingham Street to look for a furnished accommodation for me. We were shown rooms at the top of a house overlooking the river. It was a compact set of chambers, available for immediate possession.

On our way back my aunt repeated several times that this would make me firm and self-reliant. The next day, she arranged to send my clothes and books. I felt happy to have the chambers to myself but at night I was lonely with no one to talk to. I thought of Agnes and how I missed my time spent at the Wickfields.

Next day, I was delighted to receive a note from Agnes. She was in London visiting friends with her father and Uriah Heep. She desperately desired to meet me.

She met me warmly but I could sense that something was worrying her. She warned me not to be influenced by Steerforth. Then she told me that Uriah Heep had persuaded her father to take him in as his partner. She had initially thought that it would reduce the burden on her father but she had started feeling that he has started taking advantage of her helpless father.

By that time Mr. Wickfield and Uriah Heep joined us for dinner. When Agnes took her father to bed, Uriah Heep told me that he was in love with Agnes and wanted to marry her. I would never let that happen. It was evident to me that he was not in love with her but only interested in the Wickfield business.

David falls in love with lovely Dora

Chapter 15

DORA

Mr. Spenlow, my new employer invited me to his country home. He introduced me saying, 'Mr. Copperfield, my daughter Dora and my daughter, Dora's confidential friend!' I stood in front of Miss Murdstone, surprise written on my face.

Dora was the loveliest creature on earth and I fell in love with her instantly. The weekend proved to be the most beautiful period of my life. I loved Dora Spenlow to distraction! She was more than human to me. She was a Fairy, a sylph, I don't know what she was!

My reverie was broken when she asked, 'Are you very intimate with Miss Murdstone?'

'No! not at all!' I replied

'She is a tiresome creature,' said Dora, pouting. 'I don't know what papa had in mind when he chose such a bad-tempered creature to be my companion. Who wants a protector? Papa calls her my confidential friend, but she is anything but a friend! I can never dream of confiding in her! It is very hard, because I do not have a Mama! It is irritating to have such a gloomy old thing like Miss Murdstone, always following me about! I am sure Jip can protect me a great deal better. Can't you, Jip, dear?' And she nuzzled her dog with great affection. Jip seemed to understand what was being said and wagged his tail lazily.

We had a quiet day. No company, a walk, a family dinner of four, and an evening of looking over books and pictures.

I remained in this state not only on that day but day after day, from week to week and term to term. I went there, not to attend to what was going on, but to think about Dora. I was miserable to think that I had not expressed my feelings to Dora and so she had no idea of the extent of my devotion or that she cared nothing about me. I was always looking out for another invitation to Mr. Spenlow's house. It was obvious that that never came for Mr. Spenlow, like the others was oblivious to the turmoil in my heart.

Chapter 16

A LOSS

Once we were back in London, I was invited to dinner by some business friends. I heard that there was another guest by the name of Traddles. I was keen to meet him and find out more about him. Could he be the same Tommy Traddles of Salem House? When I saw him, I immediately recognized him by his hair and wide open eyes. I walked over to him and introduced myself. Both of us were equally happy to meet after such a long time and I agreed to visit his home the very next day.

It was a sloppy and untidy street. It reminded me of the time I had spent with Micawbers. Traddles told me that his parents had died, leaving behind nothing for him. He was struggling as a law student and did odd jobs to support himself. He was engaged to Sophy but their marriage will take place later. He told me that he lived with the kindest people, the Micawbers, who have had very hard times themselves. I told Traddles that I knew them and went down to meet them. The Micawbers were very glad to see me. We met with the same warmth but I realized that even now, they were very hard pressed for money.

I excused myself from having dinner there on some pretext for I had noticed that there was very little food even for the family. Instead, I invited them all to dinner at my house, next day. Next day, at my house, we were talking, eating and happily, sharing our experiences. Suddenly the door flung open and I was surprised to see Steerforth standing there. I asked him to join us for the meal which he did. Later, he handed me a letter from Peggotty. He looked preoccupied but I he did not share the reason. Even I could I not find it. After a while, he told me that he was in Yarmouth and that Emily and Ham were not yet married. Barkis was very unwell and may die any day. I told my friends that I decided to visit Peggotty.

'Why don't you come with me to Highgate, besides who knows when we meet again?' Steerforth suggested. I found that remark strange and uncalled for but went with Steerforth for a while. There his mother and her companion indirectly accused me of keeping Steerforth away from them for such a long time but I remained quiet for the reality was that he was not with me.

I reached Peggotty's house in the evening. I found Emily sitting near the fire, quiet and sad. There appeared some tension between her and Ham. Soon Peggotty came down. She looked worn out; nevertheless, she embraced me warmly and took me upstairs to meet Barkis. We spent several hours with Barkis. He opened his eyes once and stretched his hand. He said, 'Barkis is willing' and passed away. All of us were very sad for we had lost a very good human being and a dear friend!

Chapter 17

A GREATER LOSS

Mr. Barkis was buried in Blunderstone, in the same churchyard where my parents rested. Peggotty and I walked about the churchyard for an hour, after the funeral was over; and placed some young leaves on my mother's grave.

I stayed with Peggotty and helped her in all possible work. I used my knowledge and experience as a proctor, in taking charge of Mr. Barkis' will. I felt myself quite knowledgeable when I read this document aloud with all possible ceremony, and set forth its provisions to those whom they concerned. I had supposed. I examined the will with the deepest attention, pronounced it perfectly formal in all respects and thought it rather extraordinary that I knew so much.

My old nurse left with me for London the next day, on the business of the will. Emily was to stay that day at Mr. Omer's. We planned to meet in the old boathouse that night. Ham would bring Emily at the usual hour. The brother and sister would return when the day closed in at the fireside.

As planned, after our return from London, I headed for the boat house. Peggotty, Mr. Peggotty and Mrs. Gummidge were there. Ham entered after a while and gestured me to come out.

'Master Davy!' cried Ham and burst out weeping. I was shocked by the sight of such grief. I could only look at him and say, 'Ham! For heaven's sake, tell me what's the matter!'

'Master Davy! Emily, for whom I could die, has gone! Emily has run away!' said Ham and began to howl. 'What do I tell Uncle?'

Just then, Mr. Peggotty stepped out. He looked at Ham's face and knew. Ham told that Emily had left a note. She had left home to become a lady and if the man she had gone with didn't make her one, she would never return home.

'Master Davy, it is not your fault and I am not blaming you for this but his name is Steerforth and he's a damned villain!' blurted out Ham.

Mr. Peggotty uttered no cry and shed no tear. 'I'm going to seek my niece. If I had known what he was planning, I would have drowned the villain when he was in my boat. I'm a going to find my poor niece in her shame, and bring her back. No one can stop me!

Chapter 18

THE BEGINNING OF A LONG JOURNEY

The news soon spread through the town. Next
morning when I passed along the streets, I
overheard the people speaking of it. Many were very
critical of Emily, some criticized Steerforth but all had the
same sentiments of sorrow and concern for Ham and Mr.
Peggotty. Among all, respect for them in their distress
prevailed, which was full of gentleness and delicacy.

It was on the beach, that I found them— Mr. Peggotty
and Ham. They were both very grave. 'We had a detailed
discussion and decided what we need to do,' said Mr.
Peggotty to me. I'll come along with you to London
tomorrow, if it is alright with you! Ham will stay here.'

In the morning, Mr. Peggotty, my old nurse and I left
for London. Ham drew me aside and whispered, 'Mr.
Peggotty is completely shattered. He doesn't know what
he is doing or where is he going. He only knows that he
has to find Emily. I request you to be his friend!'

'Trust me, I will indeed,' said I, shaking hands with
Ham earnestly. I told Ham not to lose heart and soon
he would get his Emily back. When the journey ended,
I looked for a lodging where he could have a bed.
Mr. Peggotty wanted me to help him in meeting Mrs.
Steerforth. As I felt bound to assist him and also to

mediate, I wrote to her as mildly as I could what had happened and how I was responsible for this tragedy.

I described Mr. Peggotty as the most gentle and upright character. I ventured to request that she should not refuse to see him in his hour of crisis. I mentioned that we would reach her home at two o'clock in the afternoon. As planned, when we reached Mrs. Steerforth's house, Littimer wasn't there to receive us. Mrs. Steerforth was sitting in the drawing room and Rosa glided in, from another part of the room and stood behind her chair.

I saw Mrs. Steerforth's face and found it very pale. She looked more like her son than I had noticed earlier. She sat upright in her arm-chair, with a stately, immovable, passionless air, that it seemed as if nothing could disturb. For some moments not a word was spoken.

Then, she motioned to Mr. Peggotty to be seated. He said, in a low voice, 'I don't think that it would be right for me to sit down in this house. I'd rather stand.' And this was succeeded by another silence, which she broke somewhat like this, 'With deep regret, I say that it is a sad situation that has brought you here. What do you want me to do?'

He took out Emily's letter, unfolded it and said, 'Please read that, ma'am. That's my niece's hand!'

She read it, in the same stately and impassive way, without any display of emotions and returned it to him.

'I have come here to know, ma'am, whether he will keep his word!'

Mrs. Steerforth insults Mr. Peggotty

'No! That's impossible. He would disgrace himself. She is far below him in status! She is uneducated and ignorant.'

'Maybe she's not; maybe she is,' said Mr. Peggotty. 'I am no judge. Teach her better!'

'Since you compel me to speak bluntly, I can tell you that her humble family background would render such a thing impossible!' she replied.

'I justify nothing. I make no counter-accusations but I am sorry that is impossible. Such a marriage would irretrievably ruin my son's career and ruin his prospects! Let him forget the girl he fancies and he is welcome back. If he decides to be with her, he never shall come near me, living or dying!'

While I heard and saw the mother, I found a strong resemblance between her and Steerforth. She too had the same unyielding, wilful spirit. She rose with an air of dignity and left the room. Mr. Peggotty and I came out of the house, dejectedly and began walking slowly and thoughtfully down the hill. He told me, he meant 'to set out on his travels', that night. I asked him where he meant to go. He only answered, 'I'm a going, sir, to seek my niece. I really do not know where I will go!'

I was least inclined to leave him alone, under such circumstances but he was determined. After dinner, Mr. Peggotty took a small sum of money, barely enough, to last him for a month. He promised to communicate with me, when anything befell him. He slung his bag across his shoulder, took his hat and stick, and bade us 'Good-bye!'

Chapter 19

FROM BLISS TO SHOCK

All this time, I was madly in love with Dora.
Mr. Spenlow invited me to a picnic on Dora's
birthday. I bought a bouquet of lovely flowers for her.
It flattered me to see that she kept the flowers with her
all the while and protected them from Jip who saw
imaginary cats in them and was ready to smash them.

Four days later, Dora and I were engaged but we did
not tell her father. However, I was so happy that I had to
tell Peggotty who was still in London for the will related
work. I even wrote to Agnes about it.

One day when Peggotty and I returned to my rooms,
we were surprised to hear voices inside. When we went
in, both of us were amazed to find Aunt Betsey and Mr.
Dick there. Aunt Betsey had her cat and the birds with her
and she sat on her luggage, drinking tea. Mr. Dick stood
holding one of his big kites and had some more luggage
about him.

'My dear Aunt! What a pleasant surprise!' I exclaimed
and embraced her with great affection. I wondered if she
had learnt about my engagement with Dora or whether I
had offended her in some way. I knew I will get to know
the reason soon. Once she finished her tea, she said, 'Why
do you think I am sitting here on my luggage and why is
Mr. Dick holding on to his wonderful kite?'

I confessed that I could not guess and that I had no idea.

'Because Trot, I am ruined. This is all I have and the cottage in Dover has been rented out. We mustn't let this frighten you but I want you to be brave and self reliant.' We need to save expenses. You could make a bed for me here and find a place for Dick. I made the necessary arrangements. I took Mr. Dick to the place and he came along carrying his big kite. When I returned, I saw my aunt pacing the room. She informed me that Peggotty and she were talking about my engagement with Dora.

I replied, 'We might be very young and may appear foolish to others but both of us truly love each other.' She replied that the fondness may come to nothing but then added that there was time for all of us to recover from the losses. I thanked my aunt and went to bed. I could not sleep as I kept thinking what if Mr. Spenlow doesn't allow us to get married due to our impoverished state? I was not earning anything during my training as a proctor. I thought how I could earn something and help my aunt in her crisis.

The next day, I went to Mr. Spenlow and his partner, Mr. Jorkins and explained my financial problems to them. I also added that I will not be able to continue with the training. Neither of them offered to return the advance or to let me continue with the training. As I walked home, trying to plan for ways to overcome the crisis, a hackney cab stopped and Agnes got down. We walked together and she told me that she had heard of my aunt's financial problems and had come to meet her.

I learnt of my aunt's financial problems for the first time. She was advised by the firm of Wickfield and Heep to invest in some bank stock but the bank had failed and all the investors had lost everything.

She shared that her father and Uriah Heep were also in London. She had no private time with her father. 'There is such a change at home,' said she, 'that you would scarcely know the dear old house. Heep and his mother live with us now. He sleeps in your old room! Trot, I fear that Heep is planning some fraud or treachery against my father. I hope I am wrong but I get a very strong feeling!'

'Dear Aunt,' I interposed, 'I must do something! Join the army or go to the sea to tide over this financial crisis!'

'I won't hear of it. You are to be a proctor, if you please, sir.'

'I have been thinking, Trotwood,' said Agnes, diffidently, 'that if you have spare time, you could work in that time. Your old favourite teacher is in London and he requires a secretary to help him with his dictionary, which he is still writing. Would you mind that?'

I told her that I would love it. I wrote to Dr. Strong, requesting him for an appointment.

Just then there was a knock on the door. Agnes turned pale and said, 'I think it's papa. He promised me that he would come.'

I opened the door, and admitted not only Mr. Wickfield, but Uriah Heep. I had not seen Mr. Wickfield for some time. I was prepared for a great change in him, after what I had heard from Agnes, but his appearance shocked me.

Though still dressed with the old scrupulous cleanliness, there was an unwholesome ruddiness upon his face; his eyes were swollen and bloodshot and his hands trembled. He had not lost his good looks or his old bearing of a gentleman, but the fact that he had submitted himself to that crawling impersonation of meanness, Uriah Heep. Mr. Wickfield's dependence on him was a very painful sight to me. When he came in, he stood still until Agnes spoke softly to him, 'Papa! Here is Miss Trotwood and Trotwood, whom you have not seen for a long while!'

My aunt broke silence with her usual abruptness, 'Well, Wickfield! I have been telling your daughter how I lost money because I couldn't trust it to you. You are growing rusty in business matters. We have been discussing on this issue and I strongly think Agnes is worth the whole firm, in my opinion.'

'I fully support you, Miss Trotwood,' spoke Uriah. 'I'm aware you're nervous.'

'Go along with you, Uriah! Don't presume to say so! I am nothing of the sort. If you're a man, control your limbs and behave like one! Good God! I am not going to be serpentined and corkscrewed out of my senses!' cried out my aunt, in extreme disgust.

Mr. Heep was rather abashed by this explosion!

'I am well aware, Master Copperfield, that Miss Trotwood, though an excellent lady, has a quick temper. I only called to say that if there was anything we could do, in the present circumstances, we should be really glad to,' said Uriah and took his leave to depart. Mr. Wickfield also appeared to follow him out.

'You are not going, papa?' asked Agnes, anxiously. 'Will you not walk back with Trotwood and me?' We sat there, talking about our pleasant old Canterbury days. Mr. Wickfield, left to Agnes, soon became more like his former self; though there was a depressed look about him. Yet there was an evident pleasure in hearing us recall the little incidents of our old life, many of which he remembered very well. He said it was like those times, to be alone with Agnes and me again; and he wished to Heaven that the circumstances had never changed.

Chapter 20

ENTHUSIASM REGAINED

I began the next day with renewed vigour. I was not dispirited now. My perspective to our late misfortune had entirely changed. I had to show my aunt that her past goodness to me had not been wasted on an insensible, ungrateful person. What I had to work with a resolute and steady heart. With the new life, came new purpose. Great was the labour; priceless the reward, Dora who must be won.

My first concern was to find Dr. Strong's house. When I approached the Doctor's cottage, it was a pretty old place. I saw him walking in the garden. I opened the gate and walked up to him. He looked at me thoughtfully for a few moments and then, as he recognized me, his benevolent face expressed extraordinary pleasure, and he took me by both hands.

'Why, my dear Copperfield,' said the Doctor, 'you are a man! How do you do? I am delighted to see you. My dear Copperfield, how much you have improved! Annie will be delighted to see you. You were always her favourite!'

'My dear, your proposal is very gratifying and agreeable to me, I am sure but don't you think you could do something better than this? You are qualified for many better things good things!'

Agnes had suggested that I could help Dr. Strong with his dictionary in my spare time, without neglecting my studies. Consequently, I had written to him, proposing to help him and earn a little. I shared with him the financial problems that had befallen us and informed him that I had a profession and that I would do that work only in my spare time.

'Well, weil,' said the Doctor, 'that's true. But, my dear, what's seventy pounds a year?'

'If you will let me use the spare time that I have, in the mornings and evenings for seventy pounds a year, you will do me a great service!'

With a great deal of reservations, Dr. Strong let me start the work. So I began my busy schedule, from five in the morning to ten at night. We were to work two hours every morning, and two or three hours every night, except on Saturdays and Sundays, when I was to rest!

Mr. Dick had started to fret and worry himself out of spirits and appetite, for he could not be of much help to Aunt Betsey in her crisis. He said that he had nothing useful to do and that he was incapable of helping her. I talked to Traddles if he could help me find some useful occupation for him. He told me that he would love to use Mr. Dick's services who wrote very neatly, for copying his legal documents. He received us cordially, and soon made friends with Mr. Dick. Traddles even suggested that I learnt shorthand so that I could get a job of reporting the parliamentary debates.

'Traddles! My dear fellow! That is indeed a very good idea! I'll buy a book on stenography and master it soon.

Then I will be able to take down speeches in our court! I'll master it very soon!'

'Dear me,' said Traddles, opening his eyes, 'I had no idea you were such a determined character, Copperfield!'

During one of my visits Traddles informed me that our old friend, Mr. Micawber, whom he had been helping with several loans, had got a job as a confidential law clerk with Uriah Heep. I was amazed and disturbed for I did not trust Uriah Heep!

Chapter 21

MY DEAR DORA

By this time, we were quite settled down in Buckingham Street, where Mr. Dick continued his copying in a state of absolute felicity. My aunt, being uncommonly neat and ingenious, made many improvements in our domestic arrangements. I was the object of her constant solicitude. My poor mother herself could not have loved me better or tried to make me happy. I was indeed very grateful to her for all her love and support!

It was time for Peggotty to leave for Yarmouth. She had received no news from her brother and wanted to return to take care of Ham. Before leaving, she made me promise that if I ever needed money I would approach her.

'And, my dear!' whispered Peggotty, 'tell the pretty little angel that I would have liked to see her! Tell her that before she marries my boy, I'll come and make your house very beautiful for you, if you'll let me!' I declared that nobody else should touch it; and this gave Peggotty such delight that she went away in good spirits.

Then I went to Dora's house and without much thinking asked her if she could love a beggar because I was one. She was confused. She shook her lovely curls and laughed. I loved her childish ways but I had to make her understand. 'I am your ruined David. Are you still mine?' 'Oh yes! But don't go on with your dreadful talk of being poor!' I told her that I wouldn't but it would help her to read a few books on cooking and household accounts. My dear Dora was a lovely child, frightened of facing the real world and its problems scared her. She cried out in fright for being unprepared for domesticity. She was alarmed.

'Oh, but that's so shocking!' cried Dora.

'No, my love! Perseverance and strength of character will enable us to bear worse things. 'But I haven't got any strength at all,' said Dora, shaking her curls.

'Mr. Copperfield, I will be plain with you. Mental suffering and trial do not go with Dora. Our dearest Dora is a favourite child of nature. She is a thing of light, and airiness and joy!' added Mr. Spenlow, seeing the girl frightened and in tears.

And Dora returned, looking as lovely as before. I doubted whether she ought to be troubled with anything so ordinary. I felt like a sort of Monster who had got into a Fairy's bower and had frightened her so much to make her cry.

As I left Dora said, 'Now don't get up at five in the morning. It is so silly!' I realised that it was futile to make her realise that one must work to live. She laughed and I loved her even more!

I continued to work at my shorthand for the parliamentary debates. The shorthand symbols perplexed me. It was like learning a new alphabet.

One day, Mr. Spenlow called me to his house. When I reached, I found him walking to and fro upon the hearth-rug. He seemed very angry. Miss Murdstone was also present there.

'You have done a crooked and unbecoming action, Mr. Copperfield. When I take a gentleman to my house, no matter whether he is nineteen, or twenty-nine, I take him there in a spirit of confidence. If he abuses my confidence, he commits a dishonourable action, Mr. Copperfield.'

I feel it, sir but I never thought of the matter in this manner before. Sincerely, Mr. Spenlow, I never thought that falling in love with Miss Spenlow was improper! I genuinely love Miss Spenlow!' I assure you,' I returned. '

'Nonsense! Don't tell me on my face that you love my daughter, Mr. Copperfield!' said Mr. Spenlow, reddening.

'Have you considered your years, and my daughter's years, Mr. Copperfield? Have you considered what it is to undermine the confidence that should subsist between my daughter and me? Have you considered my daughter's station in life, the projects I may contemplate for her advancement! Have you considered anything, Mr. Copperfield?'

'Let me add Sir that we were already engaged! Your daughter loves me equally!'

'I beg of you that you will not talk to me of any such engagement, Mr. Copperfield!' stated Mr. Spenlow disdainfully.

The otherwise immovable Miss Murdstone laughed contemptuously. It was more like a snort that I heard!

Next morning, Mr. Spenlow said nothing about it in the office but before I was about to leave, he called me in, and told me that I need not make myself uneasy about Dora's happiness. He had assured her that it was all nonsense and she had nothing to say. Let me add that if you are foolish or obstinate, Mr. Copperfield, I might send my daughter abroad again. I hope you will be wise! All I desire, Mr. Copperfield, is that it should be forgotten!'

After a few days of mental turmoil, I was surprised, when I reached our office-door! Some half-dozen people were gazing at the windows which were shut up. The clerks were there. One of them said, 'This is a dreadful calamity, Mr. Copperfield. Don't you know Mr. Spenlow is dead!'

How I felt it might grieve Dora! How it made me restless to think of her weeping or being consoled by others. I asked my aunt to write a letter expressing our condolences at the loss and offering any possible help to the family.

My aunt received a letter next day. It was addressed to her but the letter inside was addressed to me. Dora was overcome by grief. She kept on thinking of her father and crying. I was keen to know how Dora would be placed, in whose guardianship would she be left. I hoped that she was not left in Miss Murdstone's care. That would the worst thing for both of us. I was also curious to know about the details of Mr. Spenlow's will for that concerned my dear Dora. It was known later that Mr. Spenlow had made no will.'

I learnt that after all the dues were settled, there wasn't even a thousand pounds for all the remaining assets. I also learnt that Dora had no other relations except two aunts, maiden sisters of Mr. Spenlow, who lived at Putney and who had chosen to stay away. These two ladies proposed to take Dora to live at Putney. Dora clung to them both, weeping and exclaimed, 'Please take Jip along with me to Putney!' So they went, very soon after the funeral.

My aunt could sense my dejection. She decided to send me to Dover to check on the tenants who had rented the cottage. Everything was fine at the cottage and on my way back, I stopped at Canterbury to meet Agnes and Mr. Wickfield. Uriah Heep's presence made me most uncomfortable. I noticed that he was constantly encouraging Mr. Wickfield to drink more than he should.

Suddenly, he blurted out, 'Mr. Wickfield, I want to make your Agnes, my Agnes! I want to marry her.' Mr. Wickfield rose from the table with a cry and seemed to go mad for a moment, pulling his hair, and shouting uncontrollably, distorted, a frightful spectacle. I put my arm round him and helped him to contain himself.

'Look at him! He has ruined my reputation! He has taken away my peace, my home and now, he dreams of marrying Agnes! Never, will I allow that!' wailed Mr. Wickfield, in agony and uncontrollable anger.

'You had better stop him, Copperfield, if you can,' cried Uriah, with his long forefinger pointing towards me. 'He'll say something for which he'll be sorry afterwards, and you'll be sorry to have heard!'

Mr. Wickfield dropped into a chair and weakly sobbed. The excitement into which he had been roused was leaving him.

Agnes caring for her father

The door opened and Agnes glided in, her face totally devoid of colour. She put her arm round her father's neck and said, 'Papa, you are not well. Come with me!'

He laid his head upon her shoulder, as if he were oppressed with heavy shame, and went out with her. Her eyes met mine for but an instant, yet I saw that she knew what had happened.

'I didn't expect he'd react like this, Master Copperfield,' said Uriah.

'But I'll be friends with him tomorrow. It's for his good.'

I kept quiet and went upstairs into the quiet room where Agnes had so often sat beside me at my books. I took a book and tried to read when Agnes joined me.

'You will leave early in the morning, Trotwood! I came to say good-bye, now!'

'Dear Agnes,' I said, 'it is presumptuous for me, who is so poor in all in which you are so rich goodness, resolution, all noble qualities to doubt or direct you; but you know how much I love you and how much I owe you. Promise me that you will never sacrifice yourself to a mistaken sense of duty, Agnes? You must never marry Uriah Heep for the sake of your father's business or for any other reason. You are too good for a creature like him!'

She smiled sadly and said, 'I must trust God!'

Chapter 22

THE WANDERER

On my return, I told my aunt what I had witnessed at Mr. Wickfield's home. I even told her that the cottage in Dover was well looked after. Then I sat down to write my letter to the two old ladies, Dora's aunts, seeking permission to meet Dora. Aunt Betsey read the letters and found them to be alright. They were posted the next morning. The reply came promptly that I could meet her on Saturdays and Sundays. I was ecstatic and threw myself into work, looking forward to spending the weekend with Dora.

I was still in this state of expectation, when I left the Doctor's one snowy night, to walk home. The noise of wheels and tread of people were hushed due to the carpet of snow. As I passed the steps of the church portico, I saw a woman's face which looked familiar. She also looked at me and disappeared in the narrow lane.

Further down, on the steps of the church, there was the stooping figure of a man, who had put down a bundle on the ground. As he stood up I was face to face with Mr. Peggotty. We shook hands heartily. At first, neither of us could speak a word.

'Master Davy!' he said, gripping me tight. 'It is so good to see you, sir. Well met, well met! I wanted to

David and Mr. Peggotty meet by accident

come and meet you but it was too late. I am going away.'
I took him to the stable yard which had some public
rooms. I found one in which a bright fire was burning. I
ordered a drink to warm us. When I saw him in the light,
I observed, that his hair was long and ragged. His face
was sun burnt. He was greyer; the lines in his face and
forehead were deeper.

With a great amount of gravity he said, 'Wherever I
have been and whatever I have seen I have not found my
little girl. He had followed Emily to France, then to Italy
and then over the mountains to Switzerland, on foot. My
dear Emily sends money to Mrs. Gummidge for me but
she gives no address. I am going to Germany for the last
letter bore that country's postmark. I watch these letters
and follow her. I will keep on doing that till I find her. I
asked Mr. Peggotty how was Ham. He told me that he
was completely shattered. He keeps himself busy in work
and takes on the toughest of tasks. That is his way of
taking grief in his stride.

Just then, I saw Martha at the door. She was the one I
had seen a few minutes back. She looked haggard but was
listening very attentively.

My dread was lest Mr. Peggotty should turn his head,
and see her too. Mr. Peggotty got up to leave. I looked at
the door but Martha was gone. Mr. Peggotty added while
leaving that he will travel ten thousand miles to find his
beloved child and if he dies on the way and if I ever met
her, I must tell Emily that her uncle died looking for her
and that he still loved her. I must also tell her that she had
been forgiven.

Everything seemed to be hushed in reverence for him, as he resumed his solitary journey through the snow.

I returned to the inn yard and looked around for Martha but there was no trace of her and the snow had covered all footprints.

Chapter 23

EVIL URIAH HEEP

I went to Putney along with Traddles to meet Dora at her aunts' house. I looked round the room for any sign of Dora but found none. Just then Jip barked in the distance and saw two dry little elderly ladies, dressed in black each resembling their brother.

'Please be seated,' said one of the ladies.

The younger appeared to be the manager of the conference, as she held my letter in her hand. They were dressed alike though the younger one wore her dress with a more youthful air which made her look more lively. They were both upright in their carriage, formal, precise, composed, and quiet.

'Mr. Copperfield, my sister, Clarissa and I have been very careful in considering this letter and have consulted our niece. We have no doubt that you like her very much.'

This gave me courage to speak most vehemently that I loved Dora better than I could tell, that my aunt, Agnes, Traddles, everyone who knew me, knew how earnest my love for Dora is!'

'Therefore we are inclined so far to accede to your request for your visits here!'

'I shall never, dear ladies,' I exclaimed, relieved of an immense load of apprehension, 'forget your kindness!'

'We shall be happy,' said Miss Clarissa, 'to see Mr. Copperfield to dinner, every Sunday, if it should suit his convenience. We dine at three and in the course of the week, we shall be happy to see Mr. Copperfield to tea. Our hour is half-past six.'

I bowed to them with immense gratitude.

Miss Lavinia then requested me to follow her. I was led to another room where I found my darling Dora, standing next to the wall in an attempt to listen. She looked beautiful in her black frock. She sobbed when she saw me. What a state of bliss I was in when Dora, Jip and I were reunited!

One thing troubled me. Her aunts regarded Dora as a pretty toy or plaything. My aunt, with whom she gradually became familiar, always called her Little Blossom. Miss Lavinia would wait upon her, curl her hair, make ornaments for her, and treat her like a pet child. They seemed to treat Dora as Dora treated Jip.

I decided to speak to Dora about this. Your aunts must treat you differently and not as a child. She made a face and began to cry but after a while, asked me to get her that cookery-book I had once spoken of and to show her how to keep accounts as I had once promised I would. I brought the volume with me on my next visit. I showed her an old housekeeping-book of my aunt's and helped her to practise housekeeping. The cookery-book made Dora's head ache, and the figures made her cry. They wouldn't add up, she said. So she rubbed them out.

Once during our walks I asked Dora, what she would do after we were married, and I should like a nice Irish stew, she replied that she would tell the servant to make it. She clapped her little hands so joyfully that I was charmed all over again.

Agnes and her father came to Dr. Strong's house to stay for a fortnight. Mr. Wickfield and Dr. Strong were old friends. As was expected, Uriah Heep followed. One night, after I had finished my work, I saw light in the study. I thought I would tell Dr. Strong not to work so hard and say good night to him. When I entered, I saw the Doctor who was visibly disturbed. He sat holding his head in his hand. For an instant, I supposed that the Doctor was ill. Mr. Wickfield, too, seemed troubled and pained. I asked them what the matter was.

Uriah Heep spoke, 'I thought it right to tell Doctor Strong what you and I have already talked about. You didn't exactly understand me, it appears! This was in response to my blank look. The moment I spoke to you the other night, you knew what I meant, Copperfield. Don't deny it! You deny it with the best intentions; but don't do it, Copperfield. I have told the Doctor about his young wife's interest in another man. I couldn't believe that Heep could be so cruel.

I knew what Uriah Heep said was untrue but Dr. Strong believed it as Annie was very pretty and much younger than him. I couldn't bear to see him in such pain. Heep was a liar and a cheat whose mission in life was to make everyone unhappy and sad.

Next he addressed Mr. Wickfield, 'Think, your Agnes is such a close friend of Annie. Would it not spoil her?'

I could control myself no longer and shouted, 'You

rascal! How dare you involve me in your evil scheme! You belong to the devil!' I struck Heep across his face. After this, I ran out of the house, very unhappy and fuming with rage.

The Doctor said that he was not well and chose to remain alone, for a considerable part of everyday, during the remainder of the visit. Agnes and her father had left a week back before we resumed our usual work. When we begun the work again, the Doctor gave me a folded note. It was addressed to me. In a few affectionate words he asked me never to refer to the subject again. I had confided it to my aunt but to no one else. I could discuss with Agnes and she did not have the least suspicion of what had passed.

Several weeks elapsed before I saw a slight change in Mrs. Strong. At first, she seemed to wonder why the Doctor spoke to her with such gentle compassion. She also wondered at his wish that she should have her mother with her to relieve the dull monotony of her life. Often, when we were at work and she was sitting by, I would see her pausing and looking at him with a sad look and her eyes full of tears.

As this change stole on Annie who was once like sunshine in the Doctor's house, the Doctor seemed to grow older in appearance and more serious. Yet, his benevolent solicitude for her, increased. A sad lull fell upon the cheerful home.

I could not think of any way to help yet we strove to do our best to bring back that happiness in their lives. Neither did my aunt, who was filled with uncertainty.

Strangely, the only real relief which seemed to make its way into this domestic unhappiness was in the form of Mr. Dick. He walked with Doctor and got him to talk. When the Doctor and I were engaged in work, he would walk with Mrs. Strong, helping her to trim her favourite flowers or weed the beds. They rarely spoke a dozen words in an hour, but his quiet interest found immediate response in both of them. He became what no one else could, a link between them.

During the Wickfields' stay, I had noticed that Uriah Heep received many business letters from his clerk, Mr. Micawber. At the same time, I also received a letter from Mrs. Micawber. She had written to me that she was very disturbed as her husband had become very distant, secretive, morose and severe. He is estranged from their eldest son and daughter, he has no pride in his twins and he looked at us all with extreme coldness. He refused to give any explanation for his distracting behaviour.

He had always a loving and caring person and the change worried her. I wrote to her that he will soon be alright but it did alarm me and set me thinking.

Chapter 24

DORA, MY WIFE

I have gained mastery in stenography and can make a respectable income by it. I am reputed for my accomplishments in all fields. With eleven others, I am reporting parliamentary debates for a newspaper. I wallow in words. I have taken to authorship. In the beginning, I wrote a little something in secret and sent it to a magazine and it was published. Since then, I am regularly paid for them. In short, I am well off!

We have moved out of Buckingham Street to a pleasant little cottage nearby. My aunt, however, does not plan to stay there but in a tiny cottage close at hand.

I have reached the legal age of twenty one and Dora and I have been given permission to get married.

I am in a dream, a flustered, happy, hurried dream. I can't believe that I am to be married the day after tomorrow. Miss Clarissa and my aunt roamed all over London to find out articles of furniture for Dora and me to look at.

Sophy arrives at the house of Dora's aunts, in due course. She has the most agreeable of faces, not very beautiful but extraordinarily pleasant. She is one of the most genial, unaffected, frank, engaging creatures I have ever seen. Traddles presents her to us with great pride.

I received Agnes from the Canterbury coach and her cheerful and beautiful face is among us for the second time. Agnes has a great liking for Traddles and it is great joy to see them meet. It was a glorious moment when Agnes was introduced to Sophy by Traddles.

I have never seen my aunt in such splendour. She is dressed in lavender-coloured silk, and has a white bonnet on. Janet has dressed her. Peggotty is ready to go to the church. Mr. Dick, who is to give my darling to me at the altar, has had his hair curled. Traddles turns up in a dazzling combination of cream and light blue. My aunt sits with my hand in hers all the way. When we stopped a little way short of the church, to put down Peggotty, she gives it a squeeze, and me a kiss.

'God bless you, Trot! My own boy never could be dearer. I have been thinking of poor dear Baby this morning.' 'So do I. I owe all of it to you. You have been wonderfully kind to me, dear aunt!'

After the marriage is solemnized, Dora and I drive away together. I awake from the dream. I believe it at last. It is my dear, dear, little wife beside me, whom I love so well!

'Are you happy now, you foolish boy?' says Dora, 'and sure you don't repent?'

I married my child wife, for Dora insists on being called that and for many months; both of us are happy. She knew little about house keeping and I was no better. We have a servant to keep house for us but we have a terrible time with her. Dinner is served late or not served at all. The meat is burnt or uncooked. Silverware has disappeared but Dora cannot scold her. I avoid arguments by not asking Dora to do anything and do whatever I can manage. Dora lives cheerfully playing with Jip. My aunt loves Dora and advises me to have patience in household chores but she is never annoyed or speaks to her about it. 'You have married a pretty and affectionate young girl. It is your duty to judge her by the qualities that she possesses and not think about the ones that she doesn't have. Try to develop them in her, with patience, if you can't, don't complain and do without them. Your future is before you. You need to solve your problems yourself and my advice is to be gentle and patient.'

Fortunately, when I was at my wits end, Peggotty came and took over the charge of the household. Her first job was to clean everything over and over again until the house became immaculate.

Although I loved Dora, at times I wished that I had married a girl with more character. I missed the companionship, where I could share my interests but Dora was very happy with the state of affairs.

A year went by and Dora seemed to lose weight and strength. My aunt and the best of nurses looked after her but her condition grew worse. I was filled with the same hollow feeling that I experienced as a child. I would carry her downstairs and I could feel that she was becoming lighter. Even when she danced with Jip, her feet were not as nimble as they used to be earlier.

Chapter 25

MR. DICK FULFILLS AUNT'S PREDICTION

It was some time now, since I had left working for the Doctor. Yet I met him frequently as we lived in the same neighbourhood.

The Doctor's desire that Annie should be entertained was most acceptable to Annie's mother for she was far fonder of pleasure than her daughter was. It was futile for Annie to protest that she was not keen for entertainment.

Annie liked being in Mr. Dick's company. 'That man had evidently an idea in his head,' said my aunt. Totally unaware of this prediction, Mr. Dick continued to communicate with the Doctor and Mrs. Strong. One night, Mr. Dick came to me when I was writing.

'Trotwood,' said Mr. Dick, 'before I sit down, I wish to make an observation. Your aunt is the most wonderful woman in the world! But for her I would have been in an asylum. Even a man like me can see clouds, the clouds between Annie and Dr. Strong. I told him in very simple words what Uriah Heep had done.

'Is the Doctor angry with her, Trotwood?' he said, after some time.

'No, in fact he is devoted to her.'

Mr. Dick sat down and looked at me for a while and then asked, 'Why can't Aunt Betsey or you help, Trot?' I told him that it was too sensitive and personal a matter for us to interfere.

'Well!' said he. 'A simple person will do what wonderful and scholarly people can't do. I will surely bring them together!'

There was no news from Mr. Dick for two weeks and I thought that he must have forgotten all about it. Then one day, while my aunt and I were visiting Dr. Strong, Mr. Dick led Annie into the study. She was pale and trembling. She sat at her husband's feet and pleaded, 'Dear husband, break this silence please! Tell me what trouble has come between us?'

The doctor tenderly took Annie's hand in his and said, 'The change in our lives is my fault but there is no change in the love and respect that I have for you!'

'Tell me what is it or tell our friends here!' and she looked at all of us, imploring to enlighten her, if they knew what upset her husband.

After a long and poignant silence I told Annie what Uriah Heep had told Dr. Strong.

When Annie heard this, she remained quiet for a while and then she spoke, 'When I was a young girl, I loved you as a father. When you wished to marry me, it surprised me but I was happy to think that you considered me worthy of being your wife. As a husband you have always been so gentle and caring that I began to love you even more. There has and never will be any other man. I have never betrayed your trust!'

The Doctor was overwhelmed and took Annie in his arms. Aunt Betsey leaned over and kissed Mr. Dick, 'You

Dr. Strong and Annie clear misunderstandings

are a remarkable man, Mr. Dick! I am truly proud of you!'

My Aunt pulled me by the sleeve and all three of us left. On my way home, I pondered how wonderfully Mr. Dick had solved the domestic issue that none of us had dared to deal with!

Chapter 26

SOME NEWS ABOUT EMILY

One evening, when I was returning home, I happened to pass by Mrs. Steerforth's house. I was called in.

'Has she been found?' asked Mrs. Steerforth, angrily.

I told her that all the while, all those who knew Emily had thought that she was with James. Mrs. Steerforth, then asked Littimer to tell me all that had happened. He narrated that after the initial excitement, James had got tired of her and suggested that she marry Littimer who was of similar social strata. Emily got really wild and had to be locked up in Naples from where she had managed to run away. Mrs. Steerforth and Rosa hoped that she would have died as they feared that she might emerge and come back in James' life. I assured them that Emily would never do such a thing. I was informed that James had been coasting Spain and had decided to engage himself in seafaring till he got tired of it.

With this piece of information, I decided to go to London where I had often seen Mr. Peggotty searching the streets for Emily. I told him all that I had learnt.

He turned pale and asked, 'Is my dear Emily alive?' I said that she certainly was and she might try to contact Martha who was also in London. Mr. Peggotty told me that he had also seen Martha and wondered why Emily would go to her? I told him that once Emily had helped Martha.

As we walked, we spotted the lonely figure of Martha going towards a desolate spot near the river. The place was a depressing and filthy garbage dump and I found no reason why Martha should go there. We followed her, convinced that she was trying to kill herself. Just as she took the leap into the murky water, I jumped ahead and caught her. She resisted and struggled to be set free. Mr. Peggotty had to assist me in controlling and holding her. When she recognized us, she stopped resisting and we led her away. She cried for a along time. I told her all about Emily.

Martha told us that she had also heard that Emily had eloped and she was worried for her sake. She said, 'Emily has always been very kind to me. When she ran away, I feared that everyone would think that my influence had corrupted her. Oh, I wish I could die and bring Emily's reputation back!' she exclaimed and began to howl again.

Mr. Peggotty told her that he had travelled far and wide to search her and he was certain that she would return to London and contact her. He added that he had forgiven her and was willing to take her home but Emily was filled with shame. He wanted Martha to help him. Martha promised to be of utmost help. Seeing her present state, I offered her some money which she refused immediately. I asked her where she could be contacted but she did not tell. I tore out a page and scribbled the two addresses where she could contact us. She left us with an assurance. Mr. Peggotty and I walked together for a while and when we parted, with a prayer for the success of this fresh effort, there was a new hope that lit his tired face.

Chapter 27

INVOLVED IN A MYSTERY

Around the same time, Traddles and I began receiving alarming letters from the Micawbers. I believed that something important lay hidden in his complex communication. The more I read the letters, the more confused they left me. I was at the height of my perplexity, when Traddles visited me.

He had come to me in an equally confused state of mind for he had received a letter from Mrs. Micawber wherein she had informed him that Mr. Micawber was going to London. She didn't know the reason which he had studiously concealed. The destination was the Golden Cross. She had requested him to meet her misguided husband and to reason with him. She had urged him to share this with no one else except you and to help solve the problem.

'I think that putting the two letters together, Copperfield,' replied Traddles, 'mean more than what they usually mean in their correspondence. Both are written in good faith, I have no doubt.'

I had often thought of the Micawbers. I recall particularly how uncomfortable Mr. Micawber was when he met me, after he became clerk to Uriah Heep. We took my aunt into confidence. She advised us to be very punctual in keeping Mr. Micawber's appointment.

When we met him, he looked preoccupied, worried and weary. When I asked if all was well, he replied, 'You are looking at the wreck of a man. I have lost my mind, my respect and sold my soul to the devil... and all this due to the deception, villainy and fraud of Heep! I cannot live like this any more. I have been under the evil spell of that serpent! I must expose that crook, Heep!'

Mr. Micawber fell into a chair in an attempt to regain his breath. He asked us all to meet him in a Canterbury hotel in a week where he would bring proof of Heep's villainy.

Chapter 28

MR. PEGGOTTY'S MISSION ACCOMPLISHED

By this time, some months had passed since we met Martha. Nothing had come of her willingness to help. Mr. Peggotty had no clue to Emily's fate. I began to sink deeper and deeper into the belief that she was dead.

Mr. Peggotty's conviction remained unchanged. He never wavered in his certainty of finding her. He did not lose his patience. The respect and honour in which I held him were exalted every day.

I was walking alone in the garden, one evening. It was a fortnight after our meeting with Mr. Micawber's week of suspense. I saw a figure at a distance, dressed in a plain cloak. It was beckoning me. 'Martha!' I exclaimed.

'Can you come with me right now? Mr. Peggotty is not at home. I left a note for him, telling him where to reach.'

We went towards London. I hired a coach and Martha gave the address to the driver. We reached Golden Square, where poor lodgings had been rented out.

We alighted at one of the entrances to the Square she had mentioned, where I directed the coach to wait. She hurried me on to one of the sombre streets. She gestured me to follow her up the common staircase. As we climbed to the top-storey, I thought I observed a female figure going up before us. As we ascended the last flight of stairs, we caught a full view of this figure pausing for a moment, at a door. Then it turned the handle and went in.

'I don't know her but she has gone into my room!' said Martha, in a whisper. I had recognized her and I was amazed at what I saw, for it was Miss Dartle!

Martha placed her hand lightly on my lips to prevent me from speaking. I could barely see Miss Dartle, or the person whom we had heard her address.

'It matters little to me Martha not being at home,' said Rosa Dartle haughtily, 'I know nothing of her. It is you I come to see.'

'Me?' replied a soft voice and a thrill went through my frame for it was Emily's!

'Yes,' returned Miss Dartle, 'I have come to look at the face that has caused so much damage. Aren't you ashamed of yourself?" She went on giving vent to the unrelenting hatred and scorn. She had placed herself in a chair. Emily was crouching on the floor before her.

'Listen to what I say!' she said; 'and reserve your false arts for your dupes. Do you hope to move me by your tears?'

'Have mercy on me! Show me some compassion or I shall die!' cried Emily

'It would be no great penance,' said Rosa Dartle, 'for your crimes! Hide yourself. Let it be in some obscure life or better still, in some obscure death! There are doorways and dust-heaps for such deaths, and such despair, find one, and take your flight to hell!'

I heard distant footsteps climbing up the stairs. I knew it was Mr. Peggotty. Within seconds, he rushed into the room.

'Uncle!' cried Emily. I paused a moment and looking in, saw him supporting her unconscious figure in his arms. He gazed for a few seconds in the face; then stooped to kiss it tenderly!

'Master Davy,' he said, in a low voice, 'I thank my Heavenly Father as my dream has come true! I thank Him for having guided me, in His own ways to my darling!'

With those words he took her up in his arms and carried her, motionless and unconscious, down the stairs.

Next morning, Mr. Peggotty visited us when Aunt and I were walking in the garden. I had already told her all that had happened the previous night. Mr. Peggotty informed us that he planned to take Emily to Australia. We shall begin our lives afresh. He asked me if I could come along with him to Yarmouth and help him in winding up his affairs at Yarmouth.

Since Dora was in good spirits in the care of my aunt, I agreed to go with him. While I visited old friends in Yarmouth, Mr. Peggotty shared his plan with his sister and Ham. The place made me think of all the lovely times I had spent in that house, how I had spent my time with Emily. I regretted bringing Steerforth there who brought sorrow to these good people. I looked for the last time the lovely bedroom where I had slept!

Chapter 29

URIAH EXPOSED

I returned from Yarmouth just in time for that mysterious appointment at Canterbury. When we reached the hotel, Mr. Micawber came to our room hurriedly and said to my aunt, 'I believe you will witness an eruption shortly. I will say that I have been in touch with Mr. Traddles for his legal advice. After five minutes, come to the office of Wickfield and Heep and ask for Agnes.' He bowed and excused himself.

After five minutes, we reached the old house of Mr. Wickfield. Mr. Micawber greeted us at the door with pretended surprise. He showed us in to the dining room. Hearing the voices, Heep came in. Our visit astounded him and he frowned. Just then, Agnes entered with her warm affable smile.

You may go, Micawber,' said Heep. When his clerk did not move, he shouted, 'Did you not hear me? Why are you waiting?'

'Because, I choose to stay and wait!' he replied without showing any emotion.

Heep turned pale and then red with anger. He screamed, 'This is some conspiracy!' Then he looked at all the faces in the room.

Traddles began to speak in a calm, business-like

manner, 'I am the agent and friend of Mr. Wickfield. I have his written permission in my pocket to act as his attorney.'

'The old idiot and ass is drunk and out of his mind. You got it from him by fraud!' screamed Heep.

'Something has been taken from him by fraud for sure, Heep and you know well what it is!'

Heep glared at each one present in the room with extreme hatred and barked, 'Copperfield, you'll make nothing of this. We understand each other, you and me. There's no love between us. Ever since you first came here, you envied me for my rise! None of your plots against me; I'll counterplot you! Micawber, you will be back on the streets!'

Totally ignoring Heep's outburst, Micawber stepped forward and gave Traddles a document which he carried in his pocket. This document proved beyond doubt, Heep's forgery of Mr. Wickfield's signature to take out all his money. As Heep's clerk, Micawber knew that Heep kept false books and charged Mr. Wickfield for bills that did not exist.

Uriah, more blue than white pounced at the letter so that he could tear it to pieces. Mr. Micawber, with great luck, noticed his move and dropped the heavy ruler on Heep's hand. It dropped at the wrist. He winced in pain as his body writhed like a serpent.

Traddles continued, 'You are to replace the money that you stole and cancel your partnership with Mr. Wickfield.

'I shall never do it!' cried Heep like a maniac. 'Then,

in that case, the law will detain you. Copperfield, get the police.

'Stop!' growled Heep, 'I'll give you everything!'

'Good! Stay in your room while we check all your papers.'

After this eruption, Mr. Micawber was back to his usual self in no time. His conscience was clear and he was happy. He shared with us that he will settle in some new city and start afresh. My aunt suggested that he could go to Australia with Mr. Peggotty and start life afresh. She even offered him the passage fare. Mr. Micawber was once again a jovial man. His wife thanked Traddles and me for all our assistance.

Traddles and Micawber confront Heep

Chapter 30

DEATH AND SILENCE

Dora continued to remain ill. The doctors told me that she would die soon. I had never dreamt that Dora would die so young.

One night she told me that it was good this way. She had failed to be the wife that I deserved. I told her that I loved her a lot and that I have been very happy with her and that she should not speak like that.

Dora asked me to call Agnes as she wished to talk to her. As my two loves talked, Jip lay at my feet. He wanted to go upstairs to Dora but I stopped him. He whined for a while and, before I could realise it, was dead. Almost at the same time, Agnes came down the stairs, her face full of pity and grief, her hands raised to Heaven, 'It's all over, Dora passed away!' she said among sobs.

I became very depressed. I thought I should die too. My Aunt suggested that I travel abroad for some time. I agreed to take the trip but first I decided that I would help Peggotty wind up his affairs and leave for Australia. I also waited only for what Mr. Micawber called the 'final pulverization of Heep.'

At Traddles' request we returned to Canterbury, my aunt, Agnes, and I. We proceeded by appointment straight to Mr. Wickfield's house where we found Traddles and Micawber behind a heap of books and journals. Mr. Dick was constantly taking care of Mr. Wickfield and he seemed more like his old self.

After a lot of paper work, Traddles determined that Mr. Wickfield had enough money to keep his business and property. This relieved Agnes immensely.

He told my aunt that her money had not been invested and lost. Heep still had it. He had taken it not for greed but because he hated David and wanted to hurt him.

'How can anyone be so mean and wicked? Thank God he has gone for good!' exclaimed aunt.

Mr. and Mrs. Micawber, was my aunt's first salutation after we were seated. 'What have you thought about that emigration proposal of mine?'

'My dear madam,' returned Mr. Micawber, ' my wife and children have welcomed your offer most graciously and look forward to starting a new life!'

'That's good news,' said my aunt.

When Peggotty heard of Dora's death, she left her brother with his last minute travel preparation to be with me. She was there with me like a pillar of support. We talked of Ham and I told Peggotty that I will go along with her to Yarmouth that very evening. Perhaps he would want me to write a letter to Emily.

As we approached the seaside town, the winds were blowing wildly. Soon the rain came down in a heavy downpour. The high waves seemed hungry to swallow the town. Yet I saw some people running towards the shore.

'A schooner from Spain! A wreck! She will go to pieces any minute.' They shouted. At that moment, a large violent wave swept men, planks and rails on the shore. No one dared to enter the raging sea when all of a sudden, I saw Ham breaking through the crowd, and running towards the sea. I ran after him to stop him but he was determined to save a man who bravely clung to the mast, the man with long dark curls and a bright red cap.

'Master David, if my time has come I will die if it hasn't I will return after saving this man! God is great!' he said.

A rope had been tied to Ham's waist. He ran into the sea but was swept back by the wave. He was hurt and bleeding but he ran back into the sea again. Just when he was close to the wreck, a high wave swept the schooner into a raging whirlpool and the people pulled on the rope and drew Ham back. He was dead.

We carried him to the nearest house where I sat near his lifeless body. A fisherman, who knew me ever since I was a child, came to the door and said, 'Sir, will you please come out with me for a moment?' I thought of the sailor who was seen clinging to the mast.

The body had been washed ashore. On the same beach where Emily and I collected shells, it was lying. It was Steerforth lying with his head on his arm as I remembered was his habit, from his school days.

I took the body to London that night. All the way I kept thinking how I would tell the mother who was already shattered. I asked the maid to give Mrs. Steerforth, my card and say no more.

The house was so still as if in anticipation of the tragic news. I could hear the girl's light step upstairs. She returned with the message that Mrs. Steerforth was an invalid and could not come down but I could meet her in her chamber.

In a few moments I stood before her. She was in his room; not in her own. I felt, that she had taken to occupy it, in remembrance of him; and that the many tokens of his old sports and accomplishments, by which she was surrounded, remained there, just as he had left them, for the same reason.

Rosa Dartle, as usual, sat in her chair. The moment she saw me she knew that I was the bearer of evil tidings. She got up so that her face was not seen by Mrs. Steerforth.

'I am sorry to observe you are in mourning, sir,' said Mrs. Steerforth.

'I have recently lost my wife,' said I.

'You are very young to know so great a loss,' she returned. 'I am grieved to hear it. I hope Time will be good to you.'

'I hope Time will be good to all of us. Dear Mrs. Steerforth, we must all have that trust in our heaviest misfortunes.'

The earnestness of my manner and the tears in my eyes, alarmed her. I tried hard to control my voice in saying his name, but it trembled. She asked if James was ill. I said that he was very ill and I motioned to Rosa that he was dead.

The old yet handsome lady sat like a stone figure.

I saw Rosa Dartle throw her hands up in the air with vehemence of despair and horror.

'Rosa!' said Mrs. Steerforth, 'come to me!'

She came, but with no sympathy or gentleness. Her eyes gleamed like fire as she confronted his mother, and broke into a frightful laugh.

'Now,' she said, 'is your pride appeased, you mad woman? Now has he made atonement to you, with his life? Do you hear?'

Mrs. Steerforth had fallen back stiffly in her chair, making no sound but a moan; cast her eyes upon her with a wide stare.

'Aye!' cried Rosa, 'look at me! Moan and groan, and look at me! Look here, at your dead child's handiwork!'

'Oh, Miss Dartle, don't be so cruel!' I said. 'The mother has lost her only son!'

'No power on earth should stop me. I have been silent all these years! I loved him better than you ever loved him!' she screamed, turning on her fiercely. 'I could have loved him, and asked no return. If I had been his wife, I could have been the slave of his! Who knows it better than I? With flashing eyes, she stamped upon the ground, most maliciously.

'Miss Dartle,' said I, 'you cannot be insensitive to this afflicted mother!'

'She has sown this. Let her moan for the harvest that she reaps today!' she retorted.

Rosa had then taken James' impassive figure in her

arms, and, still upon her knees was weeping over it, kissing it, calling to it, rocking it to and fro. No longer afraid of leaving her, I noiselessly turned back again; and alarmed the servants as I went out.

Later in the day, I returned, and we laid James' body in his mother's room. She was just the same, they told me; Miss Dartle never left her; doctors were in attendance, many things had been tried; but she lay like a statue, except for the low sound now and then. I went through the dreary house and darkened the windows. The world seemed, of late, to be so full of death and eternal silence.

Chapter 31

RETURN TO AGNES

Peggotty and I went to see off our friends. We were very happy to learn that Mr. Peggotty had decided to take Martha along with him to Australia. We told them nothing about the recent catastrophes for we did not wish to spoil their departure.

I left England soon after. For a long time, through studying and working, I had accustomed myself to robust exercise. My health, severely impaired when I left England, was quite restored. I had seen much. I had been to many countries, and I had improved my store of knowledge. I wrote with a passion and kept sending the stories to Traddles to get them published. I was becoming famous. People, I chanced to meet, had read and liked my stories. When my health had improved considerably, I decided to return to England.

I was away from home for three years and home had become very dear to me. I wrote to Agnes during these years and received letters from her, always cheerful. She told me that she had started a school for young girls. The more I thought of Agnes, the more I realised how much I loved her and how she had always been nice to me. I hoped she wasn't already married.

I landed in London on a wintry autumn evening. It was dark and raining and I saw more fog and mud in a minute than I had seen in a year. I walked for a while before I found a coach.

They expected me home before Christmas but had no idea that I would return so soon. I had purposely misled them so that I could have the pleasure of taking them by surprise. Now, I felt a chill and disappointment as no one was there to receive me. However, once I reached home, I was received by aunt, Mr. Dick and Peggotty with a lot of affection and tears. My aunt had long been re-established at Dover.

Traddles had begun his practice at the Bar, in the very first term after my departure. He had chambers in Gray's Inn, now; and had told me, in his last letters, that he was soon going to be united to the dearest girl in the world.

I was very keen to meet Traddles. I knew where to find Traddles. Number two in the Court was soon reached; and an inscription on the door-post informing me that Mr. Traddles occupied a set of chambers on the top storey, I ascended the staircase. While I was climbing upstairs, I fancied I heard a pleasant sound of laughter; not the laughter of an attorney, barrister or their clerks but of two or three merry girls.

Groping my way carefully, my heart palpitating with excitement, I reached the outer door, which had Mr. Traddles painted on it. It was open. I knocked. A considerable scuffling could be heard within but I got no response. Therefore, I knocked again.

A small sharp-looking lad, half-footboy and half-clerk, presented himself.

After a moment's inspection of me, he decided to let me in. I was admitted into a little sitting-room; where I found my old friend, seated at a table, and bending over papers.

'Good God!' cried Traddles, looking up. 'It's Copperfield!' and rushed into my arms, where I held him tight.

We cried with pleasure. 'My dearest Copperfield, my long-lost and most welcome friend, how glad I am to see you! How brown you are! Upon my life and honour, I never was so rejoiced, my beloved Copperfield, never! You have become so famous! Then he bombarded me with so many questions without waiting for an answer.

'To think, that you should come so close to the ceremony and not at the ceremony, my dear old boy!'

'What ceremony, my dear Traddles?'

'Good gracious me!' cried Traddles, 'Didn't you get my last letter?'

'No! I did not receive any letter which mentioned a ceremony!'

'Why, my dear Copperfield,' said Traddles, 'I am married!'

'Married!' I cried joyfully.

'Lord bless me, yes!' said Traddles, to my lovely Sophy! Why, my dear boy, she's behind the window curtain! Look here!'

To my amazement, Sophy emerged from her place of concealment, laughing and blushing, at the same time.

Traddles introduces his new wife, Sophy to David

I kissed her as an old acquaintance would and wished them joy with all my heart.

A few days after my return, we were sitting in the parlour when all of a sudden, my aunt asked me when I was going to visit Mr. Wickfield.

'Possibly, tomorrow, I hope but tell me is Agnes married?' I asked rather bluntly.

My aunt sat musing for a little while. Then slowly raising her eyes to mine, she said, 'I suspect she has an attachment, Trot. I can't say. I have no right to say so for she has never confided it to me. I merely suspect it.'

'She could have married when you were away but she didn't. There is only one whom she will marry!' she added with a sly smile.

'I am sure she will tell me about him tomorrow when I meet her!' I replied.

I rode to her house early next morning. I was as happy to meet Agnes and she was equally happy to meet me. Yet, I was apprehensive that she might tell me about the one she plans to marry.

I embraced her and for a little while, we were both silent. Presently we sat down, side by side; and her angel-face was turned upon me with the welcome I had dreamt of, waking and sleeping, for whole years.

She was so true, so beautiful and so good! I owed her much gratitude! She was so dear to me, that I could find no utterance for what I felt. I tried to tell her what an influence she had upon me but I simply sat and admired her serene beauty.

We spoke about the trip, about my books and experiences and of the Peggottys. When I asked her what had happened in her life, she said that Papa was recovering and was much happier. The home was quiet and happy, more like the days in the past.

'You will wait and see papa,' said Agnes, cheerfully, 'and spend the day with us? Perhaps you would love to sleep in your own room? We always call it yours.'

'I would love to do that but I have promised to ride back to my aunt's at night.' I assured her that I would do that some other day.

'I have found a pleasure,' said Agnes, smiling, 'while you have been away, in keeping everything as it used to be when we were children. For we were very happy then, I think.'

She smiled again. I took this moment to probe her about the man she would marry.

Agnes burst into tears and turned away from me, 'If I have a secret, it must remain so as it has for so many years!' she added.

'For years! And I suddenly began to understand. Should I believe that…?'

'Dear Trotwood, there is one thing I must say and I couldn't say it all the while, that I have always loved you, ever since I met you for the first time!' At that moment, we were the happiest people on earth, as we stood embracing each other.

I decided to take Agnes with me to share this good news with my aunt. Both of us embraced her from either side and told her that Emily's affection was for no one else but me. When my aunt heard this, I saw her cry hysterically for the first time. Peggotty and Mr. Dick came running into the parlour, wondering what went wrong. She gave them both a mighty hug.

Agnes and I were married within a fortnight of my return. It was a quiet little function with only the closest friends attending it. It was afterwards that Agnes told me that on the night Dora died, she had sent for her only for one reason. She had asked me, as her dying wish to take her place as my wife. Agnes wept when she told me this. I wept too, though we were both really happy.

David and Agnes have a quiet marriage

Chapter 32

VISITOR FROM AUSTRALIA

I had been happily married to Agnes for ten years. I had become a famous writer and my domestic bliss was unfathomable. One evening, while Agnes and I were sitting by the fireplace and our three children were playing in the room, I was told that a stranger wished to see me.

My servant told me that he had come for the pleasure of seeing me and had travelled a long way. He was an old man and looked like a farmer.

'Let him come in!' I instructed the servant.

There soon appeared, pausing in the dark doorway as he entered, a grey-haired old man. Little Agnes, my daughter, attracted by his looks, had run to bring him in and my wife cried out in a pleased and excited tone that it was Mr. Peggotty!

It was Mr. Peggotty. An old man now, but he was a ruddy, hearty, strong old man. When our first emotions of surprise and joy were somewhat subdued, and he sat before the fire with the children on his knees, and the blaze shining on his face, he looked, to me, as vigorous and robust, as handsome, an old man, as ever I had seen. There was no trace of sorrow on his face any more. He looked content and happy.

'Master Davy,' said he. 'It is such a joyful hour to see you with your wife and children! You were as big as the youngest of these when I first saw you!'

'A joyful hour indeed, old friend!' cried I. Time has changed me more than it has changed you since then!' said I. 'Let the dear rogues go to bed and tell me where to send for your luggage and then over a glass of Yarmouth grog, we will have the tidings of ten years!'

'I am sure you will stay with us for a couple of months! You aren't going back those thousand miles, so soon!' asked Agnes.

'Yes, I will. I have promised Emily that I will return soon. I had it in my mind to visit you and tell all about us in Australia. I am growing old you see!'

'We worked hard at first but now we are doing well with our sheep farm'.

'How is Emily?' both of us asked together.

She is as fine as can be. She heard about Ham from a traveller and was upset for a while but then resumed her work. She helps me with the farm. She had many opportunities to marry but she says that that will never happen now. Martha is married to a fine young farmer. Mr. Micawber worked at farming for several months but now is the Magistrate in our town. He is respected and loved by all. Mr. Peggotty told us, among fits of laughter, that even Mrs. Gummidge received a marriage proposal and the old woman turned it down, saying, 'I am not going to change my condition at this point of life!' In fact she put an upturned bucket over the poor fellow's head.

Mr. Peggotty stayed with us for a month. He asked
me to accompany him to Yarmouth where he wanted to
collect a tuft of grass from Ham's grave, for Emily had
made him promise that he will do that. He also wished to
meet his old friends, possibly for the last time, as he felt
that he was growing old. His eyes welled with tears when
he saw the little tablet I had put up in the churchyard
in the memory of Ham. While I was copying the plain
inscription for him at his request, I saw him stoop and
gather a tuft of grass from the grave and a little earth.

Aunt Betsey and Peggotty with David and Agnes' children

Chapter 33

IN RETROSPECT

As my story ends, I look back and see myself, with Agnes by my side, journeying along the road of life, my children and friends around us.

Here is my aunt, in spectacles, an old woman of over eighty years but upright and a steady walker of six miles at a stretch even in winters. Along with her, is my dear old nurse. Her cheeks and hands are shrivelled but she is ready to scold my children when they were wrong as she scolded me. She carries the old crocodile book from which my children read to her the way I did. My aunt's old disappointment no longer exists for she is godmother to a real living Betsey Trotwood and Dora, my second daughter, says she spoils her.

I see an old man, Mr. Dick, flying giant kites and gazing at them, along with my sons, with immense delight. He greets me rapturously.

The Doctor is struggling with the Dictionary. He has managed to reach the alphabet 'D'. Traddles is busy working at his chambers. His table is covered with thick piles of papers; and I say, as I look around me, 'If Sophy were your clerk, now, Traddles, she would have enough to do!'

'You may say that, my dear Copperfield! Those were capital days! We walk arm in arm. I am going to have a family dinner with Traddles. It is Sophy's birthday.

Traddles talks to me of the good fortune he has enjoyed.

'I have no regrets from life as I have been able to do, my dear Copperfield, all that I had desired most. I am married to the most wonderful person. I am doing well professionally, our two boys are receiving the very best education, and distinguishing themselves as steady scholars and good fellows; three of the girls, Sophy's sisters, have been married very comfortably and three more are living with us,' shared Traddles on the way home.

My lamp burns low and I have written far into the night. My charming Agnes sits beside me as I write and the children sleep soundly. I pray for this happiness for many more years.

POST-READING ACTIVITIES

1. **Discussion**
   Compare the treatment that Cinderella and David received from their step parents.

2. Write a brief sketch of the character of Steerforth and his attitude towards other people.

3. How has the concept of 'gentleman' changed since Charles Dickens' days? Does it still have bearings on the modern society?

4. **Letter Writing**
   Write a letter (imagining yourself to be David Copperfield) to your mother mentioning how much you miss her and about the ill-treatment of Mr. Creakle.

5. **Group Activity**
   Plan an awareness programme against child labour and its repercussions on society. Make posters, organize street plays and candle walks for banning child labour.

6. Prepare a travel journal giving a detailed account of David's travel after Dora's death.

About the Author
Charles Dickens

Charles Dickens was the 19th Century author of short stories, plays, novellas, novels. He is known the world over for his remarkable characters, his depictions of the social classes, and values of his times. Some consider him the spokesman for the poor and the downtrodden, for he raised awareness to their plight and misery.

Charles John Huffman Dickens was born on 7th February, 1812 in Portsmouth, Hampshire, England the son of Elizabeth née Barrow and John Dickens a clerk. John was a generous man to a fault which landed him in great debts throughout his life. When Dickens' father was transferred to Chatham in Kent County, the family settled into the genteel surroundings of a larger home.

Dickens was a voracious reader and read the works of Henry Fielding, Daniel Defoe, and Oliver Goldsmith. But in 1824, John Dickens was imprisoned for his debts. The family went with him except Charles, who was sent to work at Warren's Shoe Blacking Factory at twelve years of age.

Charles' childhood was over and he was introduced to the world of the poor, a world of child labour, harsh working conditions and at low wages. Many of his future characters like Oliver Twist, David Copperfield, and Philip Pirrip were based on his own experiences. Though Charles survived these conditions but he felt betrayed when his mother insisted that he continue working even though his father was released. However, his father arranged for him to attend the Wellington House Academy in London as a day pupil from 1824-1827.

In 1827, the Dickens were evicted from their home because they had not paid the rent and Charles had to leave school. He worked as a clerk in the law firm. In 1830, he met and fell in love with Maria Beadnell. In 1833, his first story, *A Dinner at Poplar Walk* was published in the *Monthly Magazine*.

Dickens' first book, a collection of stories titled *Sketches by Boz*, his pseudonym, was published in 1836. He married Catherine Hogarth, daughter of the editor of the *Evening Chronicle* on 2nd April, 1836. In 1836, Dickens became editor for *Bentley's Miscellany* of which *Pickwick Papers* (1836-1837) was serialised.

This marked the beginning of a successful career as a writer. Most of his earlier works were serialised in monthly magazines including *Oliver Twist, Nicholas Nickleby*, The Old *Curiosity Shop*, and *Barnaby Rudge*. These works were followed by *A Christmas Carol* (1843), *The Chimes* (1844), *The Cricket on the Hearth* (1845), The Battle of Life (1846), and *The Haunted Man* (1848).

Charles's *David Copperfield* was published in 1849 and became one of his most famous works. *Bleak House* (1852-1853), *Hard Times* (1854), and *Little Dorrit* (1855-1857) followed in the following years. In 1856 Dickens purchased Gad's Hill, his last place of residence near Rochester in Kent County.

In 1859, he founded his second weekly journal All the Year Round, the same year *A Tale of Two Cities* (1859) was first serialised. *Great Expectations* (1860-1861) was followed by *Our Mutual Friend* (1864-1865).

Charles Dickens died from a cerebral hemorrhage on 9th June 1870 at his home, Gad's Hill. To this day, his works are widely read and he is considered one of the greatest of the Victorian novelists.